US MARSHAL: JAKE HARRISON

RICHARD M BELOIN MD

authorHOUSE®

AuthorHouse™
1663 Liberty Drive
Bloomington, IN 47403
www.authorhouse.com
Phone: 1 (800) 839-8640

Published by AuthorHouse 01/30/2020

ISBN: 978-1-7283-4543-7 (sc)
ISBN: 978-1-7283-4542-0 (e)

CONTENTS

DEDICATION

This work of fiction is dedicated to four friends who cleared the path from Florida to Texas--Milton, Diane, Charlie and Jean.

BOOK ONE

JAKE

CHAPTER 1

THE EARLY YEARS

Growing up in a South Texas town of 500 people during the late 1870's was living the life of the cowboy, way before railroads and industrialization. During Jake's early childhood, he was fortunate to have an older sister as his best friend and playmate. His dad was the local sheriff and his mom was a seamstress with her own dress making shop in town. Jake's early years were pleasant, and he never went without life's essentials.

His father, Sheriff Amos Harrison, was intermittently busy as the trail drives came to Waco. The Chisolm Trail brought the herds to cross the Brazos river, and the cowboys came to the local saloons to wash down the trail dust. His mom, Erma, worked five days a week making dresses and still managed to keep house and prepare all meals. Jake was given free rein in town except when trail drives were in town.

By the age of 14, Jake was encouraged to work part time after school. Jake had already become interested in guns and shooting from practicing with his dad's supply of Colt pistols and Winchester rifles. So, when Jake went out looking for a part time job, he went straight to the local gun shop to see Mr. Bruce Carson.

Bruce was 52 years old and the son of the original senior Carson who started the shop. With a lifetime of experience and working long hours, Bruce was ready for some help in the shop. One day Jake showed up looking around the shop and making small talk with Mr. Carson.

"Well Jake, sorry I can't spend time with you today. I'm weeks behind in doing action jobs and repairing firearms."

"Ok, but that's why I'm here. I want a job

working after school and on Saturdays. In a month, school will be out for the summer, and I'll be available to work for you full time. If you spend one month training me free of your expense, I can learn to do action jobs, sales and can use your idle reloader and load ammo for you to sell. I'm a quick learner and I believe that by summer's end I will be repairing firearms. No matter what you decide, remember that I will always work on your behalf, and will always give you 110% of my effort."

Bruce was impressed with Jake's proposal and realized that this young man had a hidden presence that would make him a leader in any of his endeavors. Bruce looked at Jake and said, "You're on, I will give you a trial over the next month and if you work out, I'll pay you 50 cents on weekdays, and $1 on Saturdays."

"I accept, under one condition. In one month when I get wages, can I get a break on ammo prices so I can practice?"

"Better than that, I will give you a reloader like I have in the shop and for every bullet you reload on your own time, one comes to me and one to you. Of course, I will provide all the components to reload cases."

"Great, I'll be here tomorrow after school."

***

That summer, Amos saw his son change from childhood to a responsible young man. He went to work every day on time and came home in good spirits. He would practice shooting for one hour after supper and then reload or read about gun repairs till bedtime. In addition, Jake was showing interest in county laws and the everyday routine of a sheriff and his deputies.

By September when school restarted, Bruce had caught up in firearm repairs. With the extra action jobs and cheaply produced ammo, he was enjoying a nice profit. Jake was smart and knew how to talk to customers. People would wait till school was out to come to the shop since they wanted to deal with Jake. Bruce knew this and increased Jake's pay to 75 cents for three hours of work after schooland $1.50 for all day Saturday.

School was less interesting now that he had

a part time job and had his interest in guns. His father recognized this, but his mom had second thoughts. One day she expressed her reservations to Amos. "I feel that Jake is heading away from an academic, professional or business profession. I fear that he is heading towards a lawman profession like his dad, heh?"

"Not to be corny, but the apple usually falls close to the tree. In this day and age out west, there is plenty of criminals to keep any lawman busy. I admit that it can be a dangerous profession, but I'm willing to start training him and we'll even send him to a secondary school for lawmen. With proper training, this job can be done as safely as possible."

The next day after supper, Amos went to the range with Jake to show him the points of a fast draw. At the age of 15, he picked up the information quickly and Amos watched him for an entire hour. At the end of practice, he said, "son you have a natural talent with guns. You are fast, smooth and accurate with the Colt Peacemaker and the Winchester 73. Keep practicing and you have the potential of getting better especially with the pistol. Eventually, we'll add a shotgun and a long-range rifle to your armament."

With two more years in school to finish the 10th grade, Jake continued working for Bruce. Yet Bruce knew that Jake's days in the shop were limited. As expected, after Christmas of his last year in school, Jake quit his job and went to work as an assistant to the sheriff and his deputies. By graduation, Jake was sworn in as a full fledge 17- year-old deputy sheriff. With this title he had access to unlimited ammo for practice. By law, until he reached age 18, he could only exercise his duties if accompanied by the sheriff or one of his deputies. It was during this year that things changed in Waco.

In the pre railroad years, a trail drive arriving in the area would only stay one or two nights before moving on as soon as the herd had watered and done some grazing. They still had weeks left on the trail before getting to railheads where buyers and rail cars were waiting. Now, with the railroad in town, the railhead was here, and cattle herds were sold and shipped to Chicago slaughterhouses. That meant, that cowboys were done working, and had their pockets full of money. To accommodate them, there were bawdy houses, gambling casinos and saloons ready to take their money. The result was rowdy drunk cowboys who were angry at losing all their hard-earned wages and fighting was common—sometimes with gunfights.

Amos dreaded the arrival of each herd. It meant a lot of work till late at night, a full jail by morning, many jail pots to empty of vomitus, and the added risk to each lawman's life. Some of these cowboys were not reasonable when liquored up, and many a lawman had a gun pulled on them before they were subdued.

One famous evening was well engrained in Amos' mind. While on evening rounds, Amos and Jake stopped at the Silver King Saloon. While Amos enquired from the bartender how the evening was going, suddenly a scruffy looking character yelled out, "you have to be cheating, you just won the fifth hand in a row." Amos realized that Mr. Scruffy was now pointing his pistol at Scott Lovering, the town's head council member and merchant.

"Where I come from, we shoot card cheats," says Mr. Scruffy.

Amos spoke up, "now mister, put that gun down and we'll resolve the issue."

The outlaw knew he had a wanted "dead or alive" poster out on him and knew that the only way out of this situation was to shoot both lawmen. Jake saw the man's eyes change to evil intent. As the man turned the pistol on his dad, Amos knew he was about to die. Jake drew and shot the man between the eyes without a moment's hesitation. There was total silence in the saloon until the bartender spoke and said, "Amos, you'd better keep that son of yours close by because it's obvious you made your own bodyguard, heh?"

The next morning, Amos found a wanted poster on the dead outlaw offering $1,000 for his capture, dead or alive. He was wanted in Trinidad Colorado for bank robbery and murder. He had robbed the bank of $2000 and had killed a teller during the event. Finding only $71 in the dead man's pocket, they went to search his room at the Wilson Hotel.

They searched every nook and cranny, upturned and nearly demolished a cushioned chair and the bed. They even checked for loose floorboards—all to no avail. Finally, Amos said, "I guess we're out of luck. The money is not here."

"Yes dad, it's here. We have to think like outlaws. What is out of place in this room?"

"Nothing that I can see."

"Wrong, when was the last time you saw an outlaw bother with a shotgun, especially a beat-up rusty old shotgun?"

Jake walked over and picked up the double barrel shotgun and opened up the breech. There were two spent shells left in place. Jake pulled out the shells and found what he had been looking for. Inside both barrels were numerous tightly bound rolls of US currency in either $20 or even $100 denominations. The barrel muzzles had been packed with paper to plug them up and keep the money from falling out. After getting a cleaning rod and emptying both barrels, they counted the monies. To their surprise there was $3,200. Amos said, "We refund the bank in Trinidad and the other $1200 is yours, plus you get to keep the $1,000 reward."

The remainder of his year as a pre adult age of 17 was spent helping his dad serving papers, dragging drunken cowboys to jail, settling card game arguments, and arguing with the city council to get enough funds to maintain the sheriff's department, jail and individual wages.

The one event that upset Jake as he approached 18 was that his sister, Rose, was planning to wed a local rancher's son, George Sanders. To provide for his new wife, George was offered a ranch by his uncle in New Braunfels. The price was right, and it offered his sister a future. Yet, he would miss his sister and found the 100 miles away from Waco an insurmountable distance, even with the railroad coming soon. Life would continue but everyone agreed to get together at Christmas.

One busy day in town, the 1st National Bank was robbed of $1,500 by two thieves— the Wagner brothers. Amos quickly organized a small posse and was on hot pursuit south of town. When they reached Troy some 25 miles away from Waco, Amos cancelled the chase. When asked why he was not pursuing any further, he said, "my jurisdiction is in a 25 miles radius away from Waco. Any activities beyond that point is the responsibility of the next community. That's the law we sheriffs abide with. Only US Marshals, Texas Rangers, or bounty hunters can pursue criminals without a restrictive jurisdiction." What Amos didn't realize was how significantly this rule of law had affected Jake.

***

On Jake's 18th birthday, Amos enjoyed officially swearing in his son. Jake was now six and a half feet tall and weighed 240 pounds. He was a huge muscular man that appeared as a gentle giant. Yet, Amos knew Jake's potential in upholding the law. As the weeks rolled by, Jake ended up making his bones.

One evening a notorious gang lead by Crocker Black was spotted at Carney's Livery.

Amos had explained that he and his deputies had no duty to attempt to arrest them for just being in their town. One deputy, Ralph Kennison disagreed, and felt that as the law in town, they had the duty to risk their lives and attempt to arrest them. Amos cut off the discussion and said that he would bring up the matter with the city council.

However, a messenger arrived from Murphy's Saloon with the information that the bartender, Sam Blackwell, had been threatened at gun point, and all the patrons evicted out of the saloon. Amos said, "now this is different. A local man has been threatened and we are now dutybound to interfere and arrest these killers at all costs. Amos knew that this gang would push the lawmen in the face and force a gunfight.

Amos and Ralph armed themselves with double barrel shotguns, loaded with 00 Buckshot, but Jake preferred to rely on his Colt. While walking toward the saloon, Amos described their entry and mode of operation. By the time they arrived, the patrons were gathered on the boardwalk. One man said, "Sheriff, it's very dangerous for three of you to go against five gunfighters. Some of you will likely die in the process. Why don't you let them drink and hopefully they will leave peaceably."

Amos added, "too late for that, they threatened Sam Blackwell. Ready boys, follow me." The team did a quick entry thru the batwing doors and the two shotguns were pointed at the table of five hard men.

Amos spoke, "get up you scoundrels, you're all under arrest for aggravated assault and the depredations you've performed throughout Texas. Your bounties have gone up three times in the past year because of the deaths and mayhem you have left in your wake. Now it's the end. Give up or prepare to die. We are not going to risk our lives to bring you to jail alive. So, make your play or put your hands up."

Crocker Black knew he was at an impasse. With two shotguns pointed at his men, he knew he could over draw the youngster in front of him and even put down one lawman. He relied on his two extra men to put down the other lawman. Crocker finally spoke, "well boys, I know you can do this. We can overcome these smart asses. On the order, draw and fire!"

To no one's knowledge, a nosy newspaper reporter from the Gazette was listening and watching the saloon's event. Suddenly, Crocker Black yells, NOW. The instantaneous response was BANG, BANG, PRUT-TUT-TUT. The saloon was filled with thick acrid smoke with zero visibility. When the smoke started to settle, none of the outlaws were visible. It took a full minute to find the outlaws. The two hit by the shotguns were found 10 feet away while the three outlaws who drew against Jake were flat on their backs with a hole through each's forehead.

The outside patrons wondered what had transpired, when Sam came outside to inform them and invite them back in the saloon. The patrons asked who had shot Crocker and his two toadies. When told by Sam that, Jake's lightning fanning the pistol's hammer, was the sound they had heard. The three consecutive shots that were nearly simultaneous had accounted for the PRUT-TUT-TUT sound they had heard.

After the hubbub had settled down, Ralph checked the outlaws' pockets and recovered $529. Their pistols and gunbelts were confiscated and Ralph was sent to Carney's Livery to check the outlaws' saddlebags and lay claim to the five horses and five rifles. After the undertaker had picked up the bodies, the lawmen went back to the office.

Amos pulls out the Black's gang posters. The total was $6,000 plus $300 for the horse/saddle values, and $225 for the pistols and rifles. The grand total was over $7,000. They voted to give themselves $6,000 and to start a special bank account of $1,000, with all three lawmen's signatures on the account. These funds would be to assist the sheriff's department when the city council would refuse to cover some expenses.

The next day, the council was called to an emergency meeting requested by Amos. Once the issue of duty to arrest known gangs was presented, the discussion of three lawmen vs. four council members was a prolonged event. Eventually the council went into executive session and the three lawmen waited outside on the boardwalk. When called back inside to hear the council's decision, it was Scott Lovering who presented their recommendations.

"It is this council's unanimous opinion that our sheriff's department is dutybound to protect our citizens and maintain peace. They are not required to put their lives in danger just because there are known criminals in town as long as they don't break the law or threaten our citizens. If the sheriff or any of his deputies elect to go after these criminals, it is for the bounties they offer. In this situation, they are not protected by the council's insurance of medical care, family financial support or burial services. In this recent dutiful case, you were protected by the council's insurance and you were eligible for the bounty rewards, petty cash, firearms and horses."

With this meeting over with, he then agreed to meet with the newspaper reporter. "The reason I've agreed to meet with you is to clarify an issue before you start printing some exaggerated and flamboyant event. The problem is how you will represent the method we took down these gunfighters. Basically, we were not to put our lives in danger just to bring these men in alive. That is what the readers need to know. That way, we hope to show that we have a powerful team of lawmen who are capable of protecting this town. We hope this will help to keep outlaws and their gangs away. Please do not emphasize my son's prowess with a handgun. That would only attract every gunslinger in Texas to try his hand against Jake. And that would fill our town with the worse riffraff that mankind can offer. Of course, if you choose this latter emphasis, you and your paper will be held liable for the damage it causes."

Fortunately, the Gazette's article emphasized

a very strong sheriff's department. That contributed to an extended period of relative peace in Waco. Even the cowboys knew to cool their heels. During the year, there were so many herds arriving at the railhead that Jake suggested, that in the evenings, two lawmen should make special walk-throughs at the saloons and gambling casinos.

Starting at midnight Ralph and Jake would make rounds in the saloon district and repeat their rounds at 1 and 2AM. They would walk in every saloon and gambling casino and simply get a nod from the bartender or an owner. If there was no acknowledgement, they would approach this person and find out what the trouble was. Usually, the issue was a cowboy getting drunk, rowdy or confrontational. Bringing these individuals to jail, to sleep their drunken state off, prevented many fistfights and gunfights. In the morning, these cowboys were given a full breakfast and released.

Looking back at the reason for these late rounds' success was the fact that both Ralph and Jake were carrying sawed-off shotguns in their backpacks. According to the dime novels by Wayne Swanson and Cal Harnell, these shotguns simply had a calming effect. No cowboys in their right minds would challenge the deputies.

During the year the town remained relatively quiet. It was Amos who noticed that Jake appeared disillusioned with his life. One day, Amos decided to confront Jake with his observation. Amos said, "what is the matter Jake, you seem to be doing a lot of woolgathering these days?"

Jake realized that it was time to explain his behavior of late. "Maintaining peace in town is important, but it does nothing to stop the violent evil men that are ravaging our county and beyond. To make it worse, as the town's lawmen, we are restricted to a 25-mile radius around town. It's ironic that dogs can go wherever they want to wander, but our department has limited access. I feel the drive to be free to go after these dangerous psychopaths."

"I understand your feelings, and in this regard, you should consider applying to the

Lawman's School in Denver. After completing the course, that would make you eligible for applying to the Marshal Service in Colorado."

Jake never missed a step. With a recommendation from Amos, he applied to the Lawman's School and was accepted. However, the present class was already full and in progress. He would be entering the next class starting in 8 months.

During the next 8 months, Amos hired a replacement deputy to fill the gap anticipating Jakes departure. The new deputy, Steve Bochart, had one year's experience as a deputy sheriff in New Braunfels. Amos knew that he had had a bad experience under the leadership of Sheriff Banfield but showed a presence that convinced him he would fit in with Jake and Ralph.

One fine day at 4PM the 1st National Bank was robbed for the second time. The robbers never fired a shot, but pistol whipped a teller till President Walter House opened the vault. The team of four robbers were clearly identified as a notorious gang ravaging south Texas. Sheriff Harrison was notified by a messenger that the bank had been robbed. He thought it strange that gunshots were never heard.

Investigating the robbery, President House said that it was the Castle gang under the leadership of Buster Castle. "I am sad to say that, my old friend, Nate Sweeney was pistol whipped by Buster and is dead. In addition, they stole $3,000 in paper currency. Our bank had been hanging by a thread since the robbery last year. If we don't get this money back, we'll have to close our doors. That will mean that many townspeople will be losing their life's savings."

Amos organized a posse within 20 minutes. As they were about to leave, Jake said to Amos, "dad, you can lead this posse with Ralph and Steve and I'll stay in town to hold down the fort, heh!"

After the posse left, Jake knew the die was cast. The posse would not be able to catch up with this gang before the posse arrived at the end of its jurisdiction. It was up to Jake to save the bank, the bank's depositors, and bring some justice to Nate's elderly widow.

***

CHAPTER 2

EARLY DECISIVE EXPERIENCE

Jake walked over to Carney's Livery. "Fred, do you remember those three extra-large saddlebags I've been storing in your tack room?"

"Sure do, Jake."

"Great, would you put those on a rented pack horse and saddle my horse, I'm going after those bank robbers. I'll be back shortly after I get some trail food and my firearms. I would like to get on the trail asap."

"Both horses will be ready when you get back, be careful and be safe."

Jake had been on the trail for an hour and had amazingly covered 10 miles when he saw the posse returning. Amos rode next to Jake and said, "we caught up with that Castle gang in Troy and got into a fierce gun fight. They were waiting for us in an ambush. We lost one man and our horses ran away during the fighting. They managed to ride away at a full gallop and without horses, we had to abandon the mission. Besides we were at the end of our jurisdiction again and the posse would not follow the gang after collecting the horses."

Jake looked at his dad and said, "I expected as much. I'm going after that gang and will bring back the bank's money and the robbers will be brought to justice."

"Jake, you cannot do this with your badge."

"I know." As he hands Amos his badge, he adds, "I resign and will stay on the bounty hunting trail till it's time to enter the Lawman School in Denver."

"Ok for now, but we'll talk again when you return with the Castle gang. Good luck, be careful and don't put your life in danger. You know what I mean, heh."

Meanwhile, Buster Castle was talking to his toadies as they watered the horses. I just counted the loot and we got $3,000 from the holdup in Waco. That along with the $3,500 we got from the Ranchers's Bank in New Braunfels, we have $6,000 left over after paying $500 to that Sheriff Banfield in New Braunfeld to take his deputies on a wild goose chase out of town so we could rob the bank. That was a lucky and easy take. Plus let's not forget the other four thousand we have left over from our trip thru Nebraska and Kansas. I think it's time to hold up for a while around Austin and use the town for our entertainment.

Jake decided to continue riding the main road when darkness fell. It was a full moon and the road was good and free of chuck holes. Around midnight, he stopped to make camp and after building a cooking fire well secluded in a firepit, he made coffee and cooked beans with salt pork and biscuits. While the food was cooking, the horses were grazing and were hobbled close to camp. Jake figured he had covered 30 miles and was likely still 15 miles behind the outlaws. Knowing it was some 100 miles to the nearest town of significance, Austin, would likely be their destination to spend some of that easily earned fortune. After supper, Jake had a good night's sleep.

Jake was awakened at 5AM from his watch's alarm. He quickly had leftover biscuits and jerky and was on the trail with rested horses. It was a long day with watering stops at every opportunity and frequent greetings with passing travelers. He was getting familiar with the small dust clouds made by small groups of travelers. By late afternoon, Jake noticed a large dust cloud moving away with horses at a medium trot. It was clear that the gang had not been early on the trail since they didn't expect anyone on their backtrail.

Everything changed when the gang made

camp some 5 miles before arriving in Austin. After some serious thinking, Jake decided to find a spot to hide the horses and be high enough to observe the goings on in the Castle camp. After two days of watching them thru his 50X lens shielded binoculars; Jake established a pattern he could use. Every day after breakfast, one man would take a walk away from camp into the location of the bushes they were using. He would come back with money he would share with the other men. Then all four would leave for the day and generally come back by midnight. The next day, the pattern would repeat itself. On the second day, Jake decided to visit this source of cash.

Walking in camp with a burlap bag over his shoulder, he went in the suspicious direction. Walking slowly, he was looking for a good size rock that could be moved over a dug hole. After moving seven rocks, he found the cache. He removed the metal bear trap from the burlap bag and added the leather bag of money in the bag. After setting the trap in the path to that specific rock, he left with a smile on his face.

True to form, at midnight the gang arrived all liquored up. By morning they were back to their usual routine. Jake had spent the night with his Win 76 some 200 yards from the outlaw camp. By daylight he could follow the camp activities thru his 8X Malcolm scope on his rifle. After breakfast, the same man took his walk. This time, Jake heard the snap of the beartrap closing its jaws over the outlaw's boot. The scream that followed was enough to be heard miles away. The three other outlaws rushed to see what was going on. Arriving at the designated rock, their friend was on the ground with his boot top dangling and the jaw's teeth imbedded in the man's leg.

Two outlaws worked to free their friend who was almost in shock. Buster was seen rolling off the rock. The look on his face was rage in its true form. "Some sumbitch just robbed us and I'm going to kill him." As the two outlaws were carrying the trapped victim, Jake decided to even up the odds and shot one outlaw center mass. The outlaw went rolling backwards and Buster and the other outlaw started shooting with their Win 73 rifles. They were out of range and didn't even have a target to shoot at.

At a standoff, Jake heard Buster talking to his one man still in the game. "Harvey, we are out of range and this dude has a long-range rifle. If we try to make it out of here, he'll pick us off. Plus, he has our money and we have no choice. You go right and I'll go left. We'll both flank him and shoot him in a crossfire."

The pincer movement was in progress and Jake could spot the outlaws moving to his flanks. Jake moved his position to get control of the man coming to his right. As Buster walked three feet away from a large oak, Jake stepped out and popped Buster on back of the head with the butt of his coach shotgun. Buster collapsed but managed to fire the rifle which was at full cock. The bullet hit the ground but misled Harvey into thinking that the hunter was dead. Jake quickly applied the manacles to Buster's wrists and the ankle manacles to a short chain.

Jake got behind a boulder and waited for the man called Harvey. Harvey was walking with a smile on his face and said, "Buster where are you; did you shoot that sumbitch?" Jake stood up and surprisingly said, "No, I got him instead. Put your hands up or you'll die."

Harvey had a moment of finality, pulled up his rifle to shoot Jake, as Jake let go both barrels. The outlaw was lifted off his feet and deposited some 10 feet away, dying before he hit the ground. Jake checked the dead man's pockets and found $179 in cash which he pocketed. He picked up Harvey's and Buster's pistol rigs and rifles. Buster had $305 in his pockets. Harvey was left for the predators and buzzards. Buster was awakened with canteen water in his face and walked back to camp.

At camp, the trap victim was still unconscious. With more canteen water in the face, the outlaw awoke and again proceeded to groan in pain. Out of pity, Jack cleansed the wound and bandaged it. He didn't want this piece of crap to die of infection before the trial and hanging.

Being only 5 miles to Austin was a great temptation to deliver the two live outlaws and be done with it. Yet, Jake decided to bring the two living outlaws to Waco to stand trial.

Loading both men onto their horses, manacles were applied to one ankle and the other end locked onto the stirrup. Plus, each outlaw had his hands tied behind his back. The outlaws were given two warnings, "fall off the horse and the manacle will hold you and you'll drag, and shut up or get a whipping. Remember, I don't care one iota about you, your bodily functions or your comfort."

The first day on the trail seemed slow. At every other watering, the outlaws were remounted onto the two trailing outlaw horses, thereby resting the first two horses. At the noon break, Jake had two cans of peaches with hoecakes. When Buster and his toady both demanded they be allowed to relieve themselves, drink some water and get some food, Jake came flying off the handle. He grabbed a hardwood switch and smacked them both repeatedly in the face. Jake added, "you are no longer members of the human race, you are animals going to slaughter for the good of mankind. You pistol whipped Nate Sweeney to death, so don't expect humane treatment from me."

That night, the six horses were ground hitched on a long rope so they could graze without tangling their ropes. The two outlaws were manacled to their own tree and Jake made himself a real supper. He had coffee, canned beef stew, cheese on biscuits and canned peaches again for dessert. The night got chilly, but Jake was comfortable in his bedroll and covered with a wool blanket.

For breakfast, Jake had bacon and coffee. It took him an hour to saddle the six horses, load all the gear and the two secured outlaws. It was a long day but by 6PM, he entered town with his caravan. People started walking along the caravan till he arrived at the sheriff's office. Jake was greeted by Amos, the two deputies and President House.

"Well son, tell us what you have here." "This is Buster Castle and his toady without a name. The other two are dead. The toady needs to see Doc Fairchild, because he fell in my bear trap. I have four pistols and four rifles I confiscated, and I will also lay claim to the four outlaw horses and tack. Mr. House, here is your $3,000 and I am adding $1,500 for the first robbery a year ago. The Rancher's Bank in New Braunfels gets $3,500 and the balance of $1,500 goes to the elderly Sweeney widow. I lay claim to the petty cash I found in the outlaw's pockets or saddlebags. That comes to a total of $697. Now please throw these two outlaws in the water trough and scrub them good. They don't smell very good since they weren't wearing diapers."

That evening after a bath and a home cooked meal, Amos enquired on Jake's plans. "I checked today, and Buster has a $2,000 reward and the other three each have a $1,000 reward on their heads. I admit, this is a lot of money, but a dangerous way to get it."

"I agree, this is more money than I'm worth, but it was set by financial institutions who have lost more than the bounty I'm getting. Besides, in the future, I have plans to help my community with this money."

"So, you still have the plan of ridding our county of evil criminals and not be restricted in a jurisdiction?"

"Yes, I'm heading to Dallas. The train

will get me there in 3 hours and I'll set up headquarters in a hotel. With such a large city, I figure to get a lead on outlaw gangs. I'll wait a few days for the Western Union vouchers and deposit the money in my account. I'll only keep enough cash to live on for the next 3 weeks."

***

Jake got a ticket for himself and the two tags for his horses. Walking in the second passenger car, he took a seat in the rear of the car, naturally a defensive position with his back to the rear door that connected to the caboose. He placed his two rifles, his sawed-off shotgun, and saddlebags full of manacles on the seat next to him. He then settled down to reread selected pages of Wayne Swanson's and Cal Harnell's books on bounty hunting.

The car was nearly full, so the first passenger car was likely the same. The trip was uneventful for two hours. Without warning, two men stood, drew their guns, and announced that this was a robbery.

Both men started walking the center isle and started filling their saddlebags with purses, wallets and jewelry. Four seats in front of Jake, a satchel holder hesitated and said, "I can't give you this, it's a very important payroll which the railroad cannot lose." The outlaw smacked his pistol barrel across the man's face and pulled the satchel out of his arms. When he took the time to look in the satchel, Jake saw his chance. Jake pulled his Colt and shot the outlaw between the eyes, pushing him into his partner's arms. The other outlaw saw he was compromised, let go his partner and put his hands up in complete surrender. Jake handed manacles to the injured railroad man and had him apply them to the outlaw right wrist and secured the other end to the seat's metal frame.

Jake knew the shot would have alerted his cohorts, who were likely robbing the first car's passengers. He rushed to the front door, stepped on the outside platform and saw what was happening in the first car. A passenger had drawn a pistol, but the outlaw was quicker and shot the man in the chest. Jake never hesitated.

He jumped the car links and went smashing thru the door.

Jake shot the shooter in the pistol holding elbow and then shot his accomplice in the shoulder. Both men were out of the fight and eventually were secured to empty seats with manacles. The conductor entered, evaluated the situation, and told Jake that there was a man holding a gun on the engineer.

"Most likely to stop the train where someone would be waiting with horses. Let me have your jacket, hat and ticket pad. I'll go neutralize him."

Jake reloaded his Colt, dropped his gunbelt, and placed his pistol in the back of his pants. Rushing to the engine room as if to give news to the engineer, Jake faked his surprise to see an outlaw holding a gun on the fireman and engineer.

The outlaw yells out, "you idiot, this is a holdup. Sit your butt on the floor and shut up." Jake complied and as he was sitting down, the fireman knew that this man was not the conductor. To give Jake some cover, he smiled at him and intentionally opened the fire door too quickly. The fire flash surprised the outlaw who backed up a few steps. This gave Jake the opportunity he needed.

Jake drew his pistol and shot the outlaw in the ankle. The man collapsed to the steel floor and managed to hit his head on the engine room's steel floor. He was out cold.

Jake then asked the engineer when he had a planned stop. "I will be stopping in three miles to take water and fill the tinder with coal."

"Ok, I expect that an outlaw gang leader will be waiting with five extra horses to help his men get away. When you stop, stay down since I expect there will be some shooting when I step off the train to arrest him."

As expected, a man holding several horses was seen by the water tower. When the train came to a stop. Jake jumped off holding his sawed-off shotgun. The outlaw was surprised and drew his pistol without thinking. Jake had no choice, he let off both barrels and blew the miscreant clear off his horse.

Arriving in Dallas, the city marshal was called to the railroad yard. As he arrived with a deputy, he said, "I'm Marshal Milton Cassidy and this is Deputy Will Welch. What's this I hear of a train robbery?" The railroad man, standing next to the conductor, said, "six men tried to rob the passengers and take this $25,000 payroll for the cotton gin factory. One passenger was killed but the robbery was foiled by this brave young man, Jake Harrison. We have two dead outlaws, two badly shot up, and two live ones to deliver to you."

"Well Jake, nice to make your acquaintance, and we owe you thanks for stopping these animals." As the marshal was examining the dead outlaws, he immediately recognized one of the dead ones and said, "hey, this is Randolph Caruthers. He's a well-known gang leader that is notorious for robbing trains. That means that he and his gang members have big rewards on their heads. Let me check with Western Union and come and see me tomorrow, Jake!"

The injured railroad man added, "and our insurance will compensate the dead passenger's family as well as give a substantial reward to Mr. Harrison. By the way, thanks Jake, and my name is Nathaniel Duseldorf. Now, where are you staying while in Dallas?"

"I plan to be here 2 to 3 weeks and will be staying in a local hotel."

Nathaniel added, "I don't think so. Give this note to the manager of the RR Grand Hotel. Your stay and all your meals in the hotel's restaurant are compliments of this railroad. And if you ever need a favor, never hesitate to call on me, heh."

***

Jake walked his two horses to the nearest livery, Mel's Livery. The hostler greeted him and enquired how long he would stable his horses. Anywhere from a few days to three weeks. Here are two $20 double eagles to open my account. Give them plenty of oats, hay and have your helper exercise them. I'll check on you periodically. Oh, and would you re-shoe them?"

"You don't need to worry; I'll take good care of them. Thanks for the business and please call me Mel."

"My pleasure, and call me Jake, as well. If you need me, I'll be at the Grand Hotel registered under Harrison."

Arriving at the Grand Hotel, he gave his note to the receiving clerk. "Please show this note to the hotel manager."

The clerk stepped in the office behind the counter. A minute later, a well-dressed businessman showed up holding the note. "Sir, did you just get this note, and do you know who N. Duseldorf is?"

"Yes and no."

"Well he is third in command of the main trunk into Dallas. What kind of room do you wish?"

"I want a reading table and a water closet nearby."

"With this note, I don't dare give you anything but one of our executive suites with a bedroom, parlor, water closet and an office."

"That is not necessary, how about a single room, a table, a comfortable lounging chair and its own water closet."

"Well sir, that is all we have for rooms. If

Mr. Duseldorf comes to check, please tell him you refused a suite."

After taking a bath and changing, Jake went to supper in the restaurant. He had a tenderloin steak with so many fixings that he had to skip dessert. The coffee was superb, and he left a $1 tip after realizing that this was likely the best meal he ever had.

The next morning, he went to a local diner for breakfast since the hotel restaurant did not open till 11AM. At Lyle's Diner, he had the usual scrambled eggs, home fries, sausage and plenty of coffee. The meal cost 60 cents and he left $1 to cover the meal and tip.

Afterwards, he decided to walk thru town to see the sites. To his amazement, the town was really a city and had all the amenities anyone could ever need. The city seemed to be divided in three area—the merchant district with saloons, the industrial section with factories, and the domiciles which included private homes, boarding houses and apartments. Jake was interested in the merchant district with saloons. He walked from one end of this district to the end and back. He saw the establishments he was familiar with and new ones. He saw the usual tonsorial shop, mercantile, hardware, gun shop, dress shop, butcher, blacksmith, liveries, saddleries, feed stores, and marshal's office.

The unusual establishments included a newspaper, a garment store, a cobbler, a construction company, a buggy, wagon, and wheelwright shop, a freight office, a land office and a city clerk. The courthouse was next to a county sheriff's office. Jake would later ask Marshal Cassidy why Dallas had both a marshal and a county sheriff.

After he finished visiting, he headed to the marshal's office. Marshal Cassidy was at his desk and when Jake entered, he stood and greeted him with a smile and a handshake. "Glad to see you. I've just finished settling your finances. Let's go thru the list."

"Mel's Livery paid $400 for the six horses with saddles and saddlebags. Jameson's gun shop paid $250 for five rifles and pistol rigs. I will buy one rifle and one pistol for my deputy who needs an upgrade in firearms. The railroad gave you a lifetime pass on their railroad. The bounty rewards on all six outlaws came to an amazing $7,000. The undertaker charged $40 to bury the two dead outlaws."

"Ok, let me add, I will keep the petty cash from the outlaw's pocket for a total of $219. The ammo from the saddlebags is mine. There is no charge for the deputy's firearms. You get $200 for your trouble, and $1,000 goes to the dead teller's family, if he has any."

"That is more than generous. Thank you. Now tell us about who you are and what your plans are while in Dallas."

"I am Sheriff Harrison's son from Waco. I have been his deputy for over a year. I've applied to the Lawman School in Denver and have been accepted in the next class. So, I have eight months to pursue being a solo bounty hunter. After my training in the Lawman School, I plan to apply to the US Marshal Service. As a bounty hunter or a US Marshal, I can hunt down the worst of criminals and not be restricted to a jurisdiction. Portions of the financial rewards will be placed in a benefactor account to help the victims of violent crimes or homesteaders who are having trouble paying their bills."

"That's a commendable goal, but a very dangerous way to make a living."

"I realize that, but I'm secure in my ability to do the job. So, in this regard, I would like to propose a business arrangement with you. For your information on the outlaw activities and their whereabouts. I will give you 5% of bounty rewards I am awarded."

"Well son, you have a deal. Just so you know, half of all money I can generate while in office, goes back to the city council. That helps to pay our higher than usual salaries as city employees."

"That's great, now why do you also have a county sheriff in town?"

"As a city marshal, I am only responsible for maintaining peace and order in the city. Any criminal activity that extends out of the city is the responsibility of the sheriff. As an example, if a robbery is in progress in the city, it's my responsibility to try to stop it and arrest the robbers. Once the robbers get away, it's up to Sheriff Gerald Horne to give chase with or without a posse. The sheriff is also responsible for criminal activity in the entire county and is usually on the trail to resolve issues. Whereas, I am always in the city. I can mention that the sheriff is restricted to this county and as the outlaws leave the county, the manhunt would be available to you."

"In that case, I'll introduce myself to the sheriff and offer him the same financial deal. For now, I need some R&R and will get use to your community till a manhunt opportunity comes along. Good day and thank you."

After his meeting with Sheriff Horne, Jake opened an account in the Merchant's Bank with a sizeable deposit. He then started introducing himself to several merchants to include Cantor's Mercantile, Parker's Hardware, Walt's Tonsorial Shop, Jameson Gun Shop, and Dixie's Diner. He also visited the three saloons close to the RR Hotel, Jack's Bar, Horseshoe Saloon and Queen of Hearts Casino. These were the local businesses that he would frequent, knowing that there were many others in the city.

The days rolled on. Most days, he would

ride his horses and visit the outlying ranches and homesteads. He made it a point to stop in an isolated spot and practice shooting. He would fire 50 rounds practicing his quick draw, 50 rounds rapid rifle firing at 100-yard targets and five rounds at 400-yard targets using his scoped Win 76. In the evenings, he usually enjoyed drinking a few beers and a poker game. He even went to the Queen of Hearts Casino and tried his luck at Faro.

As comfortable as life could be, Jake yearned for some activity. He was not the type of person to sit around all day. He had a mission and wanted to get along with it. The months would be short enough, and he wanted to get started.

***

CHAPTER 3

BOUNTY HUNTING SOLO

The next day at noon, Marshal Cassidy found Jake finishing his dinner in the Grand Hotel Restaurant. Approaching Jake's table, Marshal Cassidy asked if he could join him. "Certainly, would you have some coffee, it's uniquely flavorful?"

"Thanks, I will. The reason I'm here is that Frank Cantor's Mercantile was just robbed by four rough gunfighters. They loaded $71 worth of supplies and two dozen bottles of whiskey worth another $48. The worse is that they pistol whipped him to open his safe. They took three weeks of sales income totaling $900. Frank is in trouble since he won't be able to pay his suppliers, which means that the entire town will suffer from absent inventory till he can pay his creditors."

"I'm surprised you bring this matter to me. Isn't this a job for Sheriff Horne and his deputy.

"Normally, yes. But Gerald is gone east looking for rustlers and by the time we find him, the thieves will be in the Indian Nation."

"In that case, I'd be happy to help. What direction did they go?"

"They headed north toward Plano. That is 20 miles away, and Frank pointed out that this gang had been riding hard and their horses were pretty much spent. So, I expect them to camp before arriving in Plano."

"Any idea who these desperados are?"

"Yes, I found their wanted posters and it's the Mitchum gang out of Brownsville. In the past year they have killed 7 innocent bank tellers or bank customers as well as one deputy sheriff. They are dangerous gunfighters and bank robbers with very high bounties.

"Aren't they all, heh?"

"True, but don't take any grandiose chances with these animals, they aim to kill you at all costs. This is one heartless bunch that needs to be put down like 'mad' predators they are."

"I'll pick up my other firearms and be off as soon as I get to the livery to get my horse."

"Just go upstairs to get your firearms. Your horse is outside with the manhunting saddlebags of accessories and your canteen is full of fresh water. Good luck and stay safe, or I'll never forgive myself."

***

Jake was off at a fast trot, and within 10 miles, he started smelling camp smoke. Jake stopped, tied his horse to a pine branch, changed his boots to moccasins, and brought his scoped Win 76, his sawed-off shotgun and his saddlebags. He walked about a half mile when he figured he was 300 yards from camp. With the scope adjusted to the distance, Jake could clearly see the four men in camp.

The outlaws were helping themselves to their own bottle of whiskey. Jake figured that they would drink themselves to sleep and would give him an opportunity to set up a trap.

Jake waited two hours after they were all asleep. He then crept into the camp area and found the bushes they were using for a privy. He set up a contraption which fired two shotgun shells when the trigger was activated by a loop of fine wire on the ground. Of course, there were no lead pellets in the shells, they contained rock salt. After setting the boobytrap, Jake hid 10 yards away from the sleeping outlaws, also with his sawed-off shotgun loaded with rock salt.

Two hours later, one man woke up having obvious belly cramps and needed to go to the bushes. Jake became very alert when the boobytrap contraption fired and the outlaw let out a howl to wake every animal within miles. The other three got up, grabbed their pistols, and turned toward their partner writhing on the ground, his union suit all torn up.

Jake got up, saw the three outlaws in their union suits and let go both barrels at their exposed unbuttoned back doors. The result would stay in Jakes mind forever. All three men hopped straight up like startled cats, the pistols went flying, they collapsed to the ground and kept swatting their asses as if a porcupine had grabbed hold. Finally, Jake ordered them to put their hands up and the manacles were thrown on the ground for the least burning victim to apply. All four animals were dragging their butts on the ground like a dog does to stop an anal itch. Eventually the burning partially subsided and Jake manacled each animal to their own tree, He then went to get his horse and as he arrived in camp, the outlaws were still lamenting and rubbing their buts in the grass. Jake ignored them and started preparing his breakfast.

The Mitchum gang had a nice assortment of varying foods. He chose beans, rice, cheese, bacon and Arbuckle's coffee. During breakfast, the gang leader yelled, "hey, we need some salve that I have in my saddlebags, we're burning here!"

Jake turned his back to the outlaws and continued eating his meal. Afterwards, he decided to check the outlaws' saddlebags. Jake pulled out the salve, opened the can and thru it in the fire as Mitchum yelled, "no, no, nooo." In the pants' pockets, he found $449. In the saddlebags, he found an amazing $4,799.

Jake asked, "where does all this cash come from?"

"What are you, dumb? You know our record of robbing banks throughout Texas."

"I know, but which bank does this roll come from so I can return it?"

"Ha, ha ha. For some water, I'll tell you. We've been living in luxury in San Antonio for the past six months. We've spent a lot more than that roll in your hand. I have no idea which bank this money comes from. Now how about some water?"

"Nah! Don't have any to spare."

Jake closed up camp. The outlaw packhorse had two panniers. Useless items and their clothes were burned, and the panniers were filled with gunbelts, pistols, rifles, and food. All saddlebags carried salvageable items. With the four outlaws manacled to one stirrup and both hands manacled in their backs, the caravan headed to Dallas.

Arriving in front of the marshal's office, Marshal Cassidy and Deputy Welch came outside. The look on their faces was astonishing when they noticed that the outlaw's backside union suit was missing, and the macerated butts were exposed. Marshal Cassidy asked, "What happened to these dudes, they look like they fell in a barbwire pit?"

"Oh, they woke up a grizzly and got their asses chewed up, heh!"

"I see, so this is the Mitchum gang. I have already checked, and these men have bounty rewards totaling $5,000."

"Let's bring these animals in the jail and we'll settle up. Will, better get Doc Stapleton to attend to their rears."

"I'll get the Western Union vouchers of $5,00 by tomorrow. The horses and firearms will be bought by Mel and Jameson like last time. The petty cash is yours as usual. I assume you have Cantor's $900?"

"Are you sure that the confiscated money is mine and not the robbed banks."

"I checked and the last bank robbery

performed by the Mitchum gang was over 6 months ago, so the money is yours."

"Well, in that case here is your 5% or $250 and $125 for the city council which you shouldn't have to shoulder. Give these two $20 double eagles to your deputy for the extra jailhouse watch duty till the trial. This $20 double eagle is to buy clothes for the prisoners. I will see Mr. Cantor and settle with him."

Walking into Cantor's Mercantile, Jake introduced himself. "I'm bringing your money back," as Mrs. Cantor approached the men. Jake hands Frank Cantor $1,200.

"OMG, I never thought we'd ever see a penny of that loot. But wait, you gave me too much, sir!"

"No, I gave you what was due you for your injustice. Now, how many families do you have that owe you over $50 and what is the exact total."

"Sad to say, but I have 21 homesteading families that owe me $1,342 and another 20 that are above $30 for another $639. Now you can see why recovering that stolen money was so crucial for us staying in business."

"Very good, I happen to have some extra money. Here is $2,000 to cover those accounts. I also want these families to each have a shotgun with 00 Buckshot and #4 birdshot so they can hunt and help feed themselves. I will start an account with Mr. Jameson so he can start ordering an economical double barrel shotgun and ammo. Whenever you determine that a family needs a shotgun, give them a note and send them to see Mr. Jameson. If they have a shotgun give them a box of each shell and charge it to my account."

Mrs. Cantor spoke up, "good gracious, do we tell them who is the benefactor?" "No, but I suppose the word will get out, and hopefully not before I move along."

***

A week went by and Jake started getting comfortable with poker. One evening a pot was getting rather high and Jake had three Jacks in his hand. When the pot was called, a man who had won several pots, especially high ones, showed his hand of three 10's and two

Jacks. Jake finally realized that this man was cheating and probably was a master of "slight of hands." Jake was about to confront the cheater by showing his hand, when a messenger arrived with a message for Jake.

After reading the note, Jack excused himself and stood up. As he was leaving the table, he took his cards, flipped them up on the table, and left the casino. It was days later that he found out the man was thrown out of the casino onto a horse manure pile. His winnings were separated amongst the players and a satchel of money was kept under the bar for Jake. The cheater left town the next day.

Arriving at the marshal's office, Marshal Cassidy greeted him with a fresh cup of coffee and a pastry from Lyle's Diner. Jake spoke, "Well this is a nice relief, I'm glad you sent for me since I was about to shoot a man for cheating at cards."

"Well, this is no better. I have insider information that four large plantation owners are planning preemptive activities against the black people. Since the slaves were released, many have stayed on the plantations as sharecroppers. These four owners are afraid that if the blackies start organizing, that eventually their 10% sharecropping ratio will go up and start cutting in the owner's profits."

"The result is that they have hired 3 regulators to agitate the black folks. These are nothing but killers that hire for any nefarious activity that has a price tag. In addition, they have coerced the agricultural implement salesman to organize a meeting to disrupt the blackies' gathering in their brand-new church."

"At the meeting, all attendees were paid $5. Unfortunately, those present included saddle-bums, drunks, troublemakers, the perpetually unemployed, petty thieves and underpaid street cleaners. My insider man tells me that the second meeting held yesterday was to outline a plan of attack by the regulators. This included"

- Wait till their Sunday services and throw a unlit kerosene lantern thru one window and blockade the exit doors. This is their warning.

- Throw a lit kerosene lamp in the church during services and lock the exit doors.
- Start beating blackies on the street.
- Rape some of their women.
- Or, skip burning the church and walk in to arrest a black man for raping a white woman and hang him as a vigilante organization.

"I understand the issue; how can I help you?"

"We need to stop the regulators and catch them in the act of beating or raping blackies or attempting to burn and kill black folks. If I go after these regulators, I will be perceived as supporting the black people. If you go after these killers and troublemakers, you will be perceived as simply hunting for their bounties. Once we have the regulators, we can force them to reveal who the four plantation owners are. Once we have their names, I will get a court order for their arrests if they continue organizing or supporting hate crimes against blackies."

"So, you want me to catch the regulators

in the act and bring them in alive along with witnesses. Then make them talk and give you your 5%?"

"Yes, just as simple as that, heh?"

***

Fortunately, church services were not for four days. The black folk lived on Brown Street which ran perpendicular to Main Street and opened next to Cantor's Mercantile. The men worked in the factories and the wives raised the children and took care of the house and general shopping. Until he could catch the regulators, he would patrol the corner of Brown and Main during the day to protect the black ladies. After 5PM when the factories closed, he would patrol Main Street till he got to Brown to protect black men from beatings.

On the second day, a lovely black woman came out of Brown Street and was walking to Cantors when a wagon came next to her and forced her to get in at gunpoint. Jake was watching and realized that this had to be a psychopath referred to as a regulator. The wagon slowly made its way to an abandoned shed. The woman was walked inside, bound and gagged, and stripped of her clothing.

Jake quietly entered and saw the man stimulating and preparing himself for the dirty deed. Jake sneaked up on the man and placed his pistol to the back of his head and said, "your lawless days are over, your comeuppance is just around the corner," as he popped the pistol's barrel on top of his head and knocked him flat out.

Jake released the black lady, had her get dressed and said, "I want you to go home and wait for your husband. After dark, come to Marshal Cassidy and file a complaint. Make sure no one sees you, so you remain without recognition. This man will never be free again since I suspect he is wanted for murder in another location. I doubt you will have to testify."

Jake loaded the rapist/regulator on the wagon and brought him to the marshal's office. Seeing the wagon's cargo, Marshal Cassidy commented, "this must be the rapist. Let's pull his pants up before the bible thumpers walk by and I lose a dozen future votes."

"Shucks, I was going to squirt some tomato sauce on his groin and then wake him up while holding up a bloody butcher knife."

"Damn Jake, you are getting to be a rapscallion, heh!"

After tying the miscreant to the bunk bed, Jake straddled him, opened his mouth and shoved the awl for the first time. Jake was too aggressive and shoved the awl's tip too deep and destroyed the entire nerve. Yet the result was overwhelming. Even Marshal Cassidy was holding his mouth shut and Deputy Welch was as green as a cucumber. The regulator howled, screamed and peed himself good. Withdrawing the awl, Jake said, "I think I went too deep, let me try more shallow and wiggle it more."

Finally, the regulator asked, "what in hell do you want?"

"I want to know who the four plantation owners are who hired you and started this 'Supreme White' organization of hate crimes against black people and what is your name?"

"Go to hell!"

Without hesitation, Jake shove the awl in another molar. The howling restarted but this time the regulator was mumbling something.

"What was that?"

"My name is Horace Smith and the four organizers are Sam Crenshaw, Win Snay, Octavius Morales, and Avery Argyle."

"And are you willing to testify to that fact?"

"Yes, as long as you keep that thing out of my mouth."

"Ok marshal, get that court order ready and I'll get the other two regulators."

Jake went out on Main Street and hid behind a large oak tree next to the cotton gin factory. Men came out at 5PM in droves. At 6PM a single elderly black man came out and was walking home towards Brown Street. Suddenly, a rider came around wearing a face bandana and carrying a short 2X4. Without any warning, he smacked the black man in the back. Getting off his horse, he was about to swing the cudgel a second time, when suddenly someone grabbed the piece of wood and turned it onto the assailant and broke his swinging arm. The regulator howled out and tried to hold his arm in an unnatural position. Jake smacked him on the head and knocked him out.

"Sir are you ok? Can you walk home, or do you need help?"

"I'm ok and thanks for saving my life."

"Before loading the regulator on his horse, Jake placed his foot in the broken arm's armpit and yanked hard on the man's hand. This maneuver straightened and reduced the fracture. He then threw him on his horse and brought him to the marshal's office.

"Better call Doc Stapleton again, I broke and reduced his arm. He'll need a cast."

Placing him in the next cell, Jake waved the awl to Mr. Smith and said, "what's this one's name?"

"Alan Cochran. Just so you don't have to take that thing out again, the third one's name is Tom Feldman, a real mean sumbitch!"

The next day, Crenshaw, Snay, Morales and Argyle met with

Tom Feldman. Crenshaw spoke, "Those two idiots got caught and so there is only one other thing we can do. We'll pay you $1,000 to burn the church down and lock those blackies inside."

Jake, Marshal Cassidy and Deputy Welch were hidden outside the church and Jake was certain that his preparation would neutralize this last threat. Jake had placed a modified bear trap under the only window in the church. It was camouflaged with twigs and leaves, but Jake was ready to shoot the firebomber if the trap failed, and the kerosene lantern was about to be lanced thru the window.

As expected, Feldman appeared after the religious program started. He proceeded to lock the two-exit door by tying a rope around both steel handle bars. He then lit the lamp and opened the tank's spout as he walked to the window. All three lawmen heard that infamous snap as the paddle was depressed and the jaws came to clamp on Feldman's leg. The trapped animal collapsed and threw the lit lantern behind him where it landed in the dirt road and exploded in a massive ball of fire.

The minister came to the window and asked if it was safe to continue with his sermon. Jake said, "you may want to wait till we release this animal and stick a rag in his mouth."

Getting to the jail, Jake said, "Guess you'd better call Doc Stapleton again, this dude will need stitches."

"Ok, let's settle up before the doc gets here. I checked and the bounty on these three is $4,500. Here are the three vouchers from Colorado."

"Plus, you get the usual three horses and saddles, the three pistols and rifles and the $363 in petty cash and ammo."

"You get your complete 5% and the 2.5% for the town council. Yes, from now on you get the full 5%. Your deputy gets a standard $50 as his share for the extra workload.

The next day, Marshal Cassidy met with the four organizers. He informed them that all three regulators were willing to name them as the organizers. He then showed them the court order to arrest them for hate crimes. He finished the meeting by saying that he was watching them carefully, and if he heard of similar activities against the black people, that they would be the first arrested and would be going to prison. No one spoke further and everyone quietly went their different ways.

**

For the next week, Jake was busy with two dangerous assignments delegated to him by Marshal Cassidy. Both involved dangerous outlaws with a bounty on their heads. After the second encounter and collecting some large bounties, Jake asked the marshal, "if I wasn't here, what would you do with these outlaws?"

"Nothing, I would pretend they were just another cowboy passing thru. As long as they didn't commit any serious crimes, I would leave well enough alone."

One late morning, Marshal Cassidy was waiting for Jake at Dixie's Diner. Good morning marshal, what's good on the menu. "Nothing pleases me today, and I hate to show you this telegram from an old friend in Trinidad, Colorado. City marshal, Abe Granger needs some help. Here, read it yourself:"

> **To: Marshal Milton Cassidy**
> **Dallas, Texas**
> **From: Marshal Abe Granger**
> **Trinidad, Colorado**
>
> **Have a sniper in city STOP**
> **Has 8 kills of town leaders STOP**
> **Cannot find motive or assassin STOP**
> **Need smart lawman or bounty hunter as detective STOP**
> **Will deputize bounty hunter if fits the profile STOP**

"Well marshal, this makes the task much easier. I was trying to find a way to tell you that it's time for me to move on. Since I plan to go to the Colorado Lawman School in 8 months, it is important that I spend time in Colorado. Hopefully my reputation in the state will help getting a job with the US Marshal

Service. With your recommendation, I will take the job, and proceed today to make reservations on the train."

"I will telegraph Abe today and tell him to close the position. Good luck and I hope we'll meet again."

***

CHAPTER 4

COLORADO CAPERS

Jake arrived at the railroad office to make reservations. "I would like a one-way ticket to Trinidad, Colorado."

"Well sir, that's 600 miles and at 4 cents a mile it will cost you $24. The tag for your horse will be an extra $4."

Instead of giving the clerk $28, he gave him $4 and a yellow paper—a lifetime pass. The clerk looked at the paper and said, "is this for real? I can't believe that this is signed by Mr. Duseldorf."

"Well the train doesn't leave for another two hours. Use the assigned code and telegraph it for further instructions. Meanwhile take the $28 to reserve my seat and horse tag, but I expect you'll be giving me a refund."

Jake went to the Grand Hotel for his noon dinner and closing his accommodations. He then returned to the railroad office. When the clerk spotted him, he nearly fell off his chair. Walking to the counter he said, "do all railroad clerks a huge favor. Please never tell them to telegraph that code and ask for further instructions. I swear, the answer I got back is not fit for human ears, and my clacker will never recover."

Jake boarded the train with a refund, his firearms, and a new book called, "The McWain Capers/Bounty Hunting with a wife." Per his habit, he took a seat at the rear of the car and settled in for a 20-hour ride. As he was looking at the Texas countryside, Jake wondered if he would ever return to his home-state and reside in close proximity to his parents and sister's family.

The trip was interrupted by stops in every town to disembark and take on new passengers.

Those stops were fairly quick but when railroad freight cars were exchanged, the stop would last long enough for all passengers to disembark and walk about. There were many other quick stops to take on water and coal. The longest stop was in Amarillo where all passengers took the opportunity to step off the train and find a diner for a hot meal.

After 22 hours, the train arrived at the Trinidad station. As Jake stepped onto the platform, he saw an elderly lawman holding a sign that read "Jake."

"Hello, you must be Marshal Granger, heh?"

"Yes, please call me Abe. Now what did you do to this railroad company? When I came to enquire when your train would arrive, after giving your name, the clerk turned as white as a sheet and started sweating and shaking."

"Nothing much, I just showed my lifetime pass, but the clerk could not believe it and telegraphed this code for more information. The rest is history, heh."

"I've made reservations at Willie's Livery for your horse, and for you at Mackenzie's Hotel.

It has nice accommodations and a superb restaurant. Let's drop off your horse, personal items, and firearms. Then we'll meet at my office to present the dilemma at hand."

"Great, I'm looking forward to being briefed on the matter."

***

Over freshly brewed coffee by Deputy Alan Plummer, Marshal Granger began. "What we have are 8 dead town leaders who were shot dead just before dark as they were leaving the west side. We presume they went to one of the saloons to get a drink before going home. Every man was shot in the back as he was going back to the center of town. The problem is that we cannot locate the shooter's location since there is no powder bloom that is classic with our black powder ammo. So, for a start, we need to find a motive, identify the shooter, and his shooting platform."

"Ok, starting at square one, this is going to require intensive investigative work. I will also require a legal stance in order to require interviewees to answer questions during a murder investigation."

"I agree, so, raise your right hand and I'll swear you in as a deputy city marshal."

After pinning on his badge, Jake said, "to start with, I need to walk the west side. I want to check out the storefronts and the site of each assassination."

"Fine, Deputy Plummer will go with you to answer any questions you may have."

Starting their walk, the usual merchants and business offices were the accepted norm. The business décor changed, and saloons, casinos and other bawdy houses became the new décor. Continuing their walk finally lead to boarding houses and apartment buildings. One apartment building caught Jake's eye. It was four stories with a false front.

Jake spoke, "let's walk back, I feel we missed something."

Walking past the boarding houses and saloons, Jake said, "look at that building, Hortense's House of Pleasure. Notice that it is next to the saloons. Now show me the victims' locations."

Arriving at the sites, Jake thought, *Hum, these victims' sites are all 50 yards from Hortense's bordello. Plus, the distance to that four-story apartment building is anywhere between 300 to 350 yards. A shooter on that roof would end up shooting his targets in the back.* "Ok, Deputy, let's go back to the office and chat with the marshal."

Walking back rather briskly, suddenly Jake came to an abrupt stop and stared at a business front that had not registered any significance initially. "What does that sign mean, Morrison's Research and Development?"

Deputy Plummer said, "the way I understand it, this small firm does research in developing new barrels, calibers, bullets and powders to increase the bullet's velocity. They are an independent business that sells their discoveries to large gun manufacturers such as Winchester, Remington and S & W."

"I'm going in to interview the owner. You head back to the office and ask Marshal Granger to go to the courthouse and get me a court order to interview Mr. Morrison and Madame Hortense. It would be nice if the judge also gave me a third one that leaves out the recipient's name."

"I don't think that's going to be a problem since one of the victims was the judge's brother."

***

Walking in, Jake saw five employees working at their benches. One man was standing next to a milling tool building a barrel. This fella was clearly giving Jake a furtive look. Stepping to Mr. Morrison's windowed door, Jake knocked. "Come in, what can I do for you?"

"I'm the newly appointed special deputy marshal hired to investigate the murder of your town leaders."

"I understand, how can I help you?"

"For now, until your court order arrives, tell me what you do here."

"We are working on creating a new gunpowder that will push bullets above 2000 fps. This being way above the safe velocity of lead bullets, which is +-1500 fps, we are also experimenting with different lead bullet coatings. Right now, we are using a copper sheath over the bullet. On top of all this, we are using smaller calibers and are presently experimenting with the 32 caliber."

"This is all very interesting and I hope you succeed. But I'm only interested in this new gunpowder. Does it create a powder bloom?"

"No. Unlike black powder, this new powder, called white powder or smokeless powder, is clean. It has no powder bloom and does not require the cleaning of burnt gunpowder residue which can corrode a barrel and ruin it."

"What is the chemical composition of each powder?"

"I fail to see how the chemistry of gun powder can help you find the assassin. Anyways, that is a trade secret and is going to require a court order."

"Agree, how about a cup of coffee while we wait."

"Guess, I have no choice. Step into my office."

By the time the coffee was ready, Deputy Plummer arrived with the three court orders he had requested. He hands one to Mr. Morrison and waits. "Very well, in full disclosure I shall start. Black powder is made up of sulfur, charcoal, and potassium nitrate. Smokeless powder is made up of insoluble and soluble nitro cellulose with traces of ether and paraffin."

"I know what black powder looks like, so can I see a sample of smokeless powder so I can recognize it, which is what I meant instead of the chemical composition, sorry!"

"How many barrels have you made to experiment with this new 32 caliber bullet?"

"Six."

"May I see them?".

"Of course, follow me." Arriving at a gun-safe, Morrison uses his key and opens the safe's steel door. Jake looked inside and said, "why do I only see five?"

Morrison was visibly shaken. Jake suggested that he relock the safe and step into his office for further talks. Jake again noted the furtive look from the same worker.

"Please keep the missing rifle quiet. I assume that all your workers have keys to access the rifles. So, I need the names and addresses of those 5 workers. Please continue business as usual, but keep in mind that one of your employees could be an assassin."

***

His next stop was Hortense's House of Pleasure. As he entered the receiving area, Jake was amazed at the beautiful Victorian furniture and décor. He was alone, so he rang the bell for service. A well dressed and endowed lady appeared. "May I speak to Madame Hortense?"

"I am she; how may I be of service?"

"I'm Deputy Marshal Harrison and I would like to ask you some questions regarding your clientele and the recent murders."

"Sorry, but that is private information and I cannot help you without a court order."

"This will satisfy your legal responsibility." As he hands her the court order signed by Judge Whitaker. Madame Hortense carefully reads the order and says, "Very well, let's move to my private office."

"Now deputy, what do you wish to know?"

"I have a list of five names, would you tell me if any of these men are your clients?"

"Yes, this one, Avery Cochran. He had been a regular visitor, but we have not seen him in the past 6 weeks."

"Any idea why he has not returned."

"During his last visit, he severely beat my girl, and was asked to never return for services."

"Was this a recurring problem."

"No, apparently he accused my girl of giving him some kind of illness. So, I had her checked by Doc Whitcomb and he gave her a clean bill of health. So, whatever he had, he got it somewhere else."

"The second list I have is the names of the 8 murdered gents. Were these your customers?"

Looking at the list, she lifted her head and said, "Yes, they were all regulars. Am I in some legal difficulty?"

"I don't think so Ma'am. My report to the marshal will reflect this. Thank you for your help."

***

His next stop was the 4-story apartment building. Arriving, he noticed that Avery

Cochran's address matched the apartment that he was looking at. The entrance lobby had a directory and Cochran's name matched the only 4th floor apartment.

Walking up the steps to the top floor, he knocked but he knew no one would answer since Cochran was at work till 5PM. Jake took out a unique tool that allowed picking the lock and open the door. Walking in he could not find anything unusual except for an empty medicine bottle labeled "Balsam of Copaiba" and a half empty bottle of Magnesium Hydroxide. As he was leaving, he spotted a closet door that was locked. Using his pick, he opened the door. Inside was an 1885 highwall in 32 caliber and topped with an 8X Malcolm scope. Next to it was an ammo belt with unusual bullet tips made of copper instead of lead. Jake closed the closet door and exited the apartment.

As Jake was walking back to the marshal's office, he thought. *The information from Hortense and Morrison is circumstantial. Finding the missing gun is inadmissible because I entered illegally. Besides, Cochran could always say he borrowed it to do some more research with it. I need more solid documentation, or I need to catch the sniper in the act. I think I will use my last court order and visit with Doc Whitcomb. I need to find a motive for such grievous acts.*

***

Doc's waiting room had two patients ahead, so Jake took a pad and started writing his report to Marshal Granger. Once in the office, Jake said, "I'm Deputy Marshal Harrison and I'm investigating the 8 murders that have plagued your city. I need to talk to you about one of your patients, and before you object, I have a court order signed by your judge, Judge Whitaker. This will release you of all liability."

Reading the document, Doc said, "What would you like to know?"

"To start, what is Balsam of Copaiba and Magnesium Hydroxide?"

"The Copaiba is an extract from a South American tree that is used to treat the 'Clap' and the Magnesium is to settle the stomach from the Copaiba's side effects."

"I see. Did you treat Avery Cochran with this medicine?"

"Yes, but the treatment failed, and I had to use a more aggressive treatment to clear him."

"What treatment was that?"

"It is a heat treatment. I heat a flexible stylus in a water bath to 110 degrees Fahrenheit and then insert it in the affected penis to cook the diseased penis lining and prostate. It is not pleasant, and some men do not tolerate it very well."

"Was Cochran one who did not do well?"

"Yes, he yelled and screamed, and threatened to tie me up and repeat the treatment on me. When he demanded that I remove the wire, as he called the stylus, I told him that he still had two minutes till the treatment finished. At that point he yelled so loud that he emptied my waiting room."

"That explains why he beat one of Madame Hortense's gals."

"My next question regards the 8 murdered victims. Did you do an autopsy on them?"

"Only a modified one, I removed the bullets only since the cause of death was obvious."

"May I see them?"

"Certainly, I may say they were unusual. The caliber was a rare 32 and the bullets were lead, coated with copper."

"Yes, they are as expected. Thank you for your time. Please keep this name quiet, for this may be our murderer. We don't want to alert him of my investigation."

***

His final stop was Marshal Granger's office. Meeting with the marshal and his deputy, he said, "this is what I have so far." Jake went over the meetings and visits. "Morrison's facts include the new caliber, new ammo, new smokeless powder and the missing test rifle. Hortense's facts include the encounter with Avery Cochran beating a working girl, and the admission that all dead victims were customers."

"The visit with Doc Whitcomb confirms that Cochran suffered from the 'clap' and had endured a painful treatment which he blamed on Hortense's House of Pleasure—and that's his motive. The modified autopsies also confirmed the copper plated 32 caliber bullet."

"Of course, the smoking gun found in Cochran's apartment cannot be entered as evidence since I entered without a warrant."

Deputy Plummer interjected, "I'm missing something. Why does blaming a whorehouse provide Cochran a motive for 8 murders?"

"I meant; Cochran figured that the working girl gave him a venereal disease which she would have caught from customers. So, Cochran shoots customers as his revenge. A bit warped, but consistent with a sick mind, heh."

Marshal Granger added his summary, "the information from Morrison, Hortense and Doc Whitcomb are all very good but are all circumstantial evidences. The illegal entry cannot be used unless we repeat the break-in with a warrant and a witness. However, any smart lawyer can wipe out the circumstantial evidence and imply that Cochran had the new rifle home to do more testing at the range but forgot to sign it out. So, we need a smoking gun to prevent Cochran from getting off on technicalities. Despite this, you did a very nice investigation."

"So, after an investigation is completed, it is up to the prosecutor to use the facts and circumstantial evidence to convict the culprit—assuming the defense attorney is not smarter than the prosecutor. Otherwise we hope to get an admission of guilt from the accused or we catch the culprit in the act."

"Yes, and in this case, you aren't going to get an admission of guilt and any prosecutor would hesitate to bring formal charges against this suspected guilty party."

"Thank you and I agree; I will be watching his rooftop every evening till dark and all-day weekends. I will catch him in the act. Let's hope it's not after his next victim is dead, heh."

***

Jake got permission from the owner of that three-floor hotel, The Mackenzie Hotel, across the street from the Cochran's apartment. Jake had a room on the third floor, and with an access key, had easy entry to the roof. With a setup of a chair, rifle rest, and long-range scoped Win 1876, Jake hid behind the hotel's false front and waited. Three nights in a row he spotted Cochran coming home after work and nothing happened. However, after 5PM, many businessmen came on the street to enter at Hortense's bordello and leave an hour later to walk back toward Main Street. Jake thought, *it's not so far-fetched to think that one of those businessmen may have left some disease at the unsuspecting ladies of the night. In any event, I hope I'm not barking at the wrong tree by putting all my eggs in one basket—by going after Cochran."*

Friday night was the fourth night of standing guard. Jake realized that if nothing happened tonight, that it would be a long vigil to spend all of Saturday and Sunday sitting on a hot roof from noon to 8PM.

At 7PM, Jake noticed some movement on the apartment's roof. By using his hand binoculars, he recognized Cochran setting himself up behind the roof's parapet with a chair, gun rest and that 1885 high wall rifle with the 8X Malcolm scope. Everything happened quickly.

Jake saw a well-dressed man exit the bordello and Cochran stood up with his rifle in the gun rest. The barrel barely cleared the parapet as Cochran was seen eyeing his target.

As quick as Jake could react, he placed the rifle to his shoulder, saw Cochran in his scope's cross hairs, and squeezed the trigger with determination. Two loud bangs in quick succession were heard. Cochran stood up and Jake saw his facial expression, the look of a surprised rat in a rat trap. Cochran then fell onto the parapet and rocked over the edge with the rifle. The body crashing on the boardwalk broke several planks and Jake knew Cochran was dead. Before descending to the street, Jake saw the assassin's target holding his right arm. It was obvious that the man had not received a fatal wound.

Running down the hotel's stairs, Jake ran to check that Cochran was dead. He had a fatal gunshot to the chest and his neck was broken during the four-story fall. Cochran was laying on his back with his neck at a strange angle. It made Jake wonder if he had seen death come as he was falling to the ground since his face showed a look of total disbelief and shock—now caught in the throes of death for eternity.

People were coming to see what was going on. Jake saw Madame Hortense, Doc Whitcomb, Mr. Morrison, Marshal Granger, Deputy Plummer, and a man holding his bloodied arm. The man spoke up and said, "I don't know who you are deputy, but I owe you my life. My name is Emmitt Powell from San Antonio. I own the Circle P Ranch and if you ever need a favor, don't hesitate to call on me." "My pleasure sir, my name is Deputy Jake Harrison."

***

The next day, Jake was having an early supper at the Mackenzie Hotel's Restaurant when Marshal Granger came to say hello and added, "I came to settle some finances with you."

"You don't owe me a thing, Marshal Cassidy in Dallas asked me to come help you, and when I agreed to do so, I was not aware there was a bounty involved."

"This is not a bounty; this is a reward put

up by the cattlemen and coal mining executives who had lost several good men to this assassin. So, here is a bank draft for $5,000 with a thanks from me for stopping that madman. In addition, Emmitt Powell came to my office this morning. After I explained how you had investigated the 8 murders and identified the likely shooter, Mr. Powell opened his billfold and gave me $1,000 in cash to give you as his thanks. I don't think I've ever held so much paper currency in my hands." BANG…. BANG…BANG-BANG.

"What in hell was that?"

"Those shots came from way the other end of town—where the Merchant's Bank is located"

On a full run, Jake and Marshal Granger arrived at the bank to find people up in arms. The bank president, Thomas Glassman, described what happened. "We've been robbed of $20,000 in cash and two men are dead, the first is one of my tellers and the other is this crying lady's husband. We are ruined!"

Emmitt Powell added, "if this money is not recovered, I'm also ruined. I came to town to pay for a herd of Hereford and Durham beef stock originally purchased to crossbreed with Texas Longhorns. I had $10,000 wire transferred here a week ago so I could make my purchases. Now I have nothing." Marshall granger asked, "how many outlaws were involved and does anyone have an idea what the gang's name is?"

President Glassman said, "there were five in the bank and one holding the horses. One of my clerks identified two of them as the Wagner brothers who were the ones giving orders."

The word Wagner brought Jake into the picture. "Marshal, I know who these men are. They robbed my hometown bank in Waco of $1,500 and we could not give chase since they rode beyond our jurisdiction. This will again happen here, by the time you get a posse organized, this bunch of animals will be out of your jurisdiction as it happened to my dad a few years ago. Let me go after them. I'll bring them back alive and will bring back your money. You have my word on that."

There was silence and it was Emmitt Powell who spoke first. "This young man shows an amazing strong presence; I feel we should let him go. What say you Marshal?"

"No doubts, Jake get your horse, gear and firearms."

The livery man, Willie, spoke up. "Here you go. As I heard the gunshots, I saddled Jake's horse, trail gear and his firearms."

Jake didn't waste a minute, he hopped up in the saddle and was out of town at a full gallop.

***

Jake was tracking the outlaws. They were on the main road heading north towards the coal mining towns of Ludlow, Walsenburg, and Colorado City before the next big city of Pueblo. Ludlow was 15 miles away and Jake figured they would camp just outside of town. Their next bank heist would likely be late afternoon tomorrow in Ludlow. Jake knew he would need to stop them tonight.

Trailing the gang was made easy by the lack of rain for the past two weeks. The road was dry and running horses would raise a dust cloud. Jake would stay three miles behind the gang to maintain visibility. After hours of trailing this bunch, the outlaws were seen veering off the road. They traveled one-hour cross-country till they chose a spot and set up camp. Jake rode at a walk to within a mile; staying concealed by trees and tall brush. He ground hitched his horse on a long tether to allow him to crop some grass and have plenty of water. With his long-range Win 76 he was ready for a long-range rifle gunfight, and with his shotgun, he was armed for a close gunfight. He then took his boots off and put his moccasins on. Grabbing his last item, was the saddlebag with his jungle warfare contraptions.

Once he found himself within 300 yards, he had to make a decision. He had two choices. The first, he could start shooting long-range at the outlaws and likely kill most of them. The second, he could wait till dark, when the outlaws would get all liquored up and fall asleep in their stupor. Since he had promised to bring the bulk of this gang in alive, he chose the second method.

Hours later, the outlaws were all out and

asleep in their union suits and under blankets in the cool night air. That is when Jake snuck up to the outlaw's camp and went to the horse's roped corral. He covered the path with 4 X 4-inch boards that had a 3-inch nail sticking out of the board. The board was covered with dirt to hide it from view. With the booby traps all set, he then applied some hot pepper to each of the outlaw horses' noses. He then ran back to the sleeping outlaws' camp and waited.

The outlaw horses started to whinny, snort and raise all sorts of noises. The outlaws all woke up and Wagner yelled to Slim to go check on the horses. Suddenly there was a scream and a curse from hell. Slim yelled so loud that all the outlaws got up and headed for the horses to see what was wrong with Slim. In the process, another outlaw stepped on a nail and collapsed to the ground screaming holy hell.

Happy to see two gunfighters out of commission, Jake yelled out, "put your hands up, you are all under arrest for murder and bank robbery. I have a double barrel sawed-off shotgun on you and will shoot anyone who points a gun at me."

Without warning, the only outlaw who had a gun in his hand turned and was about to shoot Jake when the shotgun went off. The outlaw and his pistol went flying out in the bushes. "Now no one has a gun so get on your bellies and put your hands behind your backs."

Jake opened his saddlebag and took out five wrist manacles and applied each one, including the two animals with a nail protruding from their feet. Once the manacles were applied, the two impaled outlaws demanded the nail be pulled out. Jake stepped up to do the deed to the first man and said, "this may hurt since the nail is jagged to stay impaled"—as he yanks the board and tears the nail out of his foot. The outlaw never bothered screaming since he had passed out.

Jake then moved to the other impaled outlaw. The outlaw tried to sneak away and kept saying NO..NO..NOooooh. "You psychopaths kill and destroy families without remorse. And you think I'm going to be gentle with you, heh?"

Jake pulled the nail out with pieces of bone and muscle. The outlaw vomited and dry heaved repeatedly but never lost consciousness.

After changing each outlaw's manacles to secure each outlaw to his own tree, Jake then rebuilt the fire and went to sleep till morning. By daylight, Jake used the outlaw's supplies and cooked himself a grand breakfast of bacon, beans, eggs, buttered grilled bread and plenty of coffee. One Wagner leader said, "We all need some water and need to pee. Some food would also be nice." Jake interrupted his meal, stepped to Wagner, and kicked him in the mouth. "Shoe leather is all you'll get from me. Don't ever speak again, the next time you do, it will be a piece of firewood that will change your face forever."

After breakfast, Jake went to check out the dead outlaw. He picked up his pistol. In camp, Jake went thru the outlaws' pants pockets and saddlebags. He collected six pistols and six rifles and an amazing $30,000 in US currency from the saddlebags. In the pants pockets, he collected $581. Jake sat down after counting the money and was totally perplexed. He thought, *how many people died and how many victims lost their loved ones. The result is ruined lives. On top of that, who will help these families. Victims are easily forgotten after the funerals are done with. Jake knew he had the financial base to help these victims over the short and long term.*

***

Arriving back in Trinidad was like a circus coming to town. People were walking along the caravan of trailed horses carrying weather beaten outlaws tied up with their hands manacled in their backs and a foot securely tied to a stirrup. Stopping at the bank, Marshal Granger commented how two of the outlaws had a hole in their foot. Jake shrugged it off by saying that they had accidentally stepped on a nail in the Colorado forest. Marshal Grange lifted his eyebrows and smiled.

Stepping out of the Merchant's Bank, President Glassman came to greet Jake. After entering the president's office Jake said, "here is your $20,00 you lost. Marshall Granger, please send $1,500 to my dad, Sheriff Harrison, to return the money stolen from our hometown bank. Now did your elderly teller have any family?"

"No, he was a lifelong bachelor."

"What about the crying young lady who lost her man?"

"That was Mrs. Natalie Coombs."

"Here is $2,000 and start a bank account in her name. Give me the paperwork and bank drafts in her name." Jake finished the day by depositing the balance of some $6,500 in his own bank account.

The next day, Jake was busy selling the outlaws' horses, pistols and rifles. When he was done with that, he went to see Natalie Coombs. After introductions were made, the teary-eyed young girl said, "we were just married, and my husband had a good job working for the hardware store. Now I'm a nineteen-year-old widow with no income or profession."

"Stop there, here is enough money to support yourself till you remarry or buy a business. I suggest you consider buying a diner. I saw a for sale sign at Butch's Diner and it appears to include an apartment upstairs. Make him an offer and work with him a couple of months before taking ownership. *Jake was thinking of his dime novels by Swanson and Harnell about it being wiser for victims to find a way to support themselves instead of relying on the benefactor fund, time after time.*

That evening before supper, Deputy Plummer came to get Jake, for a meeting with Marshal Granger. "Jake, it's time to settle finances. I have Western Union vouchers totaling $1,500 for each Wagner brother, and $500 each for all their four men. That totals $5,000."

"Thanks, and here is $500 for you and your deputy, for your help and allowing me to go after those outlaws."

"Well thanks, and what are your plans for the future."

"It's the middle of June and I start the Lawman School on September 1st. I think it's time I establish a reputation in Colorado seeing that I'm planning to apply to the US Marshal Service by January. I'm planning to ride the 200 miles to Denver and maybe take on some bounty hunting manhunts on the way. There is always plenty of work available to guarantee the law will be upheld. I can always take on a short term deputy sheriff's job along the way. Either way, I build my reputation and experience which will likely ease my application to the US Marshal Service."

"Well, stay safe. Always keep in mind that you are not to put your life on the line, just to avoid killing a murderer. The only way to continue your travels and reach your goals is to stay alive. Now, if you need a recommendation when applying to the US Marshal Service, I'd be glad to write one. Just send me a telegram. Goodbye young man."

The next morning, while preparing to leave, a man in a business suit came to see Jake at the livery.

"My name is Norman Rainville, I'm the banker responsible for delivering the payroll to several coal mines from here to Pueblo to include mines in Ludlow, Walsenburg, and Colorado City. The payroll is going by local stagecoach from each local bank to each mine.

The problem is that we have many highwaymen that are robbing the stagecoach. I want to hire you to bring these outlaws to justice. The pay is $100 a day plus whatever bounty is on their heads. You can also sell their horses and firearms. We mean business, since without a payroll, thousands of good folks will be out of work. So. What say you?"

***

CHAPTER 5

LAWMAN SCHOOL

Mr. Rainville, I'm interested. Please tell me why it is that your stagecoach cannot fight off the outlaws or escape from their guns?"

"The stagecoach cannot escape when the outlaws shoot one of the horses pulling the coach. By doing an emergency stop with a horse dragging, the coach is left in the open with a bunch of shootists picking off the guards from the protection of trees or boulders. We need to deliver the payroll by another means, or we need to rid the roads of these robbers, or both."

"It appears you are correct. By doing this, your stagecoaches will carry mail and passengers to the mines. This will then free them as bait for outlaws. I will ride the roads with the payroll in my saddlebags and will arrest those who would waylay me. Make sure you leak this fact to all your bank and stagecoach employees."

Jake organized the next three weeks. Each week he would patrol the road from the local bank to the mines. The first week were the roads out of Ludlow, the second was out of Walsenburg and the third was in and out of Colorado City—gold ore coming in and payroll out.

Jake dressed himself in a fancy riding suit to appear as an unarmed businessman. His pistol was in a pommel holster hooked to the saddle horn and covered with a thin leather flap that hid the entire pistol and holster. On his first day out, Jake had a confrontation that was classic of all future encounters. Moving at a slow trot, he saw four riders approaching. Each rider was well healed and riding a quality horse.

Today, Jake stopped and waited for the riders to approach. "Howdy, where you cowboys heading and what's your business?"

The lead man responded, "Our business is you. Being well dressed as you are likely means you are carrying money," as he pulled his pistol he added, "so fork it over if you want to live."

"Well, I can't do that." As he pulled open his vest to show his badge, he added, "you see, I'm carrying a mine payroll and I'm arresting you for attempted robbery and murder."

"Those are mighty big words for a dandy not even armed." As the outlaw pulled back his hammer, Jake pulled his pistol from the pommel and shot the armed outlaw between the eyes, violently knocking him off his horse. The other three outlaws saw themselves under the gun and simply put their hands up.

The story then became a repetition. Jake brought the dead and living outlaws back to town. He would collect their bounty, sell their firearms and horses, make a bank deposit and go back on the road to rid the area of more waylaying outlaws. By the time he had cleaned all the roads, he had collected $29,000 in three weeks' time.

After special thanks from Sheriff Keith Stratton covering Ludlow and Walsenburg and

Marshal Garrett Galvin in Colorado City, Jake continued his northern trek to Denver.

***

After a day to cover the 25 miles from Colorado City to Pueblo, Jake decided to visit with the local lawman, Marshal McAllister and Deputy Cavill. After introduction were made, Marshal Preston admitted that there had not been any major crimes in the area for some time. However, he did admit, at the deputy's urging, that there was an outlaw gang, whose leader was named Desmond, that was in town to kill him.

"It appears that I sent his brother to Huntsville for raping a 'minor' gal. Apparently, he didn't survive in prison as children rapists often don't. I sent for the US Marshals yesterday but got an answer that they couldn't get here for four days. I don't know why I'm telling you all this, since this is not your fight."

"How many are there?" "Five."

"Are these wanted men?"

"Yes, from what I can tell, all five are wanted

for murder incurred during bank robberies throughout Colorado. That's why I asked for US Marshal assistance."

"If you and your deputy are willing to put down the two end gunfighters with a shouldered shotgun, I will take down the middle three!"

"Are you sure you are capable of outdrawing three gunfighters? These are roughnecks that love to kill."

"I'm secure with my ability, and I've done it before. So, stop worrying and let's go arrest this seditious bunch of piss-ants."

Deputy Cavill added, "I've heard talk of this man's ability with a handgun. He has laid a trail from Dallas to Colorado City. I trust him, so let's do it Marshal."

"Ok, load up the two shotguns. We'll find them at Kingston's Saloon."

Arriving at the saloon, the bartender was outside sweeping the boardwalk. "Gus, tell the Desmond gang that I'm here to arrest them. Either they come out in the street or I'm coming in and you'll have a gunfight in your bar."

"Yes Sheriff, they'll be coming out."

Stepping out, Desmond says, "you don't present a real threat with your deputy and a boy." Addressing Jake, "you can leave and live, this is your only chance."

"Well, I can't do that since I promised the marshal that I would help him arrest you. We will kill you if you draw against us."

At that point, the marshal and his deputy lifted their loaded shotgun to their shoulders. Desmond added, "we're all very fast draws and we'll put you three down."

Without warning, Desmond yells, "NOW." The result was devastating. The shotguns roared and three pistol shots were heard in rapid succession at a speed faster than a Gatling gun. All five outlaws were on the ground with their pistols at their sides.

After settling the finances to cover bounties and the sale of firearms and horses, Jake signed over two of the bounties to Marshal McAllister and Deputy Cavill for their part in the arrest. With thanks, Jake went back on the road after several nights sleeping in a real bed and enjoying the diner's home cooked meals.

His next two stops involved assisting Sheriff Henry Buckland in Colorado Springs and Sheriff Joshua Claybourne in Castle Rock. The problem was a common one. Outlaw gangs were hiding in plain sight wherever there were limited lawmen. The reality was that no sheriff with one deputy could ever go against gangs of five or more outlaws. In both situations, the outlaws were in saloons drinking, playing cards or getting serviced by the saloon girls.

Jake used the same method to arrest these gangs. He would enter the saloon and order a beer. After enquiring where the outlaws were seated, Jake finished guzzling his beer as he casually walked toward the proper table. When close enough, he smashed his beer mug on top of the nearest outlaw's head, and then swung the mug to the next man on his right. By the time the other outlaws realized what was happening, Jake had his Colt drawn and the hammer pulled back. After his usual line, "put your hands up or die," the potential gunfight was defused, and the sheriff and his deputy entered with the manacles.

These last two arrests had yielded large bounties, extra petty cash, and the usual sale of firearms and horses. Jake took a room in Castle Rock for a week to settle financial matters, open a bank account and rest before entering the Lawman School. During this time, he sold his horse, saddle, and cooking utensils.

The next day, he did a financial accounting of his total income accumulated since leaving Waco. To his embarrassment, he had $89,993 divided in several banks. He never totaled the amount already disbursed to victims of violent crimes and others in need.

In a large carpetbag, he packed his extra clothing and his personal care items to include soap, razor, shaving mug, toothbrush/powder and comb. In one saddlebag he had his jungle warfare paraphernalia. The other held his ammo, bounty hunting books, compass, 50X binoculars, sewing kit, bullet forceps, and carbolic acid to sterilize wounds.

The last items coming with him were his firearms: Colt in 44-40, Win 73 also in 44-40, Win 76 in 45-70, Webley Bulldog/shoulder and belt holster in 44 Rimfire, and his sawed-off 12-gauge shotgun in a backpack holster. Plus, a gun cleaning and maintenance kit.

The day before leaving for Denver, he withdrew $2,500 in large bills and $200 in small bills. The $2,500 was to open an account in the First National Bank of Denver and the $200 was for pocket cash. He then went to the nearest mercantile and purchased a new set of clothes, hat and boots.

The next morning, he boarded the train for a 30-mile ride to Denver. He chose to be armed with his Bulldog in a shoulder holster under his vest—a more acceptable décor in the big city.

***

Arriving at the Denver rail yard, Jake took a taxi to bring his gear and firearms to the Lawman School. After a 10-minute ride, the school came into view. It comprised of five multi-storied buildings, a barn, and a shooting range. The driver was instructed to head to the admissions' building where his belongings were unloaded. Paying the cabby $1, he entered the admissions' building and walked into a receiving parlor. "Welcome sir, how may I help you?"

"My name is Jake Harrison and I'm here to join the fall class for lawmen."

"Yes, I see your name. Go ahead and bring your luggage to the dormitory/bunkhouse. Choose a bunk and place your gear in the closet next to your bunk. That will be your personal space for the next four months. Registration starts a 1PM today—bring cash or bank drafts to pay for services till graduation, heh?"

When Jake entered the three-story bunkhouse, the first floor was nearly full of new students. There was only one bunk left and Jake took it. Next to his bunk was a young black man. Jake went over and said, "I'm Jake Harrison" and extended his hand. The black man stood and shook his hand saying, "and I'm Willie Irving."

"Pleased to meet you. How about if we share some of our backgrounds."

"Sure, mine is simple. I was born and raised in Louisiana on a homesteading farm. For the past year, I worked as a deputy sheriff and now I'm here to improve my skills and knowledge for a better job. How about you?'

"I was born and raised in Waco Texas. By age 18, I was proficient in quick draw, point shooting, short range speed rifle, and long-range rifle shooting. My dad was the local sheriff and I spent one year as his deputy. In the past eight months, I've been a solo bounty hunter. My goal is the US Marshal Service which is why I'm spending four months in this school since it's a very valuable stepping-stone to the Marshal Service."

"I hear that attendance is soon to be a requirement for applying to the Marshal Service. Why did you become a bounty hunter instead of staying on as a deputy sheriff?"

"I wanted to be free of jurisdictions when on a manhunt of violent evil outlaws. At the same time, although a dangerous lifestyle, it was a financially rewarding eight months."

"Really, well I've been poor all my life and we'll have to talk about bounty hunting again."

"Ok, well it's close to 1PM, shall we get in line for registration?"

The school's enrollment was topped at 50 students and the 100-day program was given three times a year. It served a half dozen western states and provided training for private lawmen as well as more advanced police forces.

The total fee was $600. The breakdown included $300 for tuition, $100 for housing, $100 for three meals a day, and $100 for unlimited ammo. Jake paid with a local bank draft. Willie was next to register and as he stepped up, he told the registrar that he had been told the total fee was $500.

"We had a price increase to compensate for higher operating costs."

"Well, I'll skip the meal plan and will find an evening job to pay for my meals."

Jake stepped in and said, "nonsense, here is a bank draft to cover your meal plan, you're here to learn, not work."

Willie was so surprised that he moved off the line, fully realizing that a white man had just extended a friendship hand.

After registering, they walked back to the bunkhouse and Willie said, "I consider this a loan and will pay you back some day."

"Willie, I have more money than I'll ever need. This is a gift and here is $100 in cash for spending money. And let's never talk about money again, OK?" Willie was still flummoxed and simply nodded his head in agreement.

***

That evening, the school's Commandant, Dutton Peabody, gave his introductory remarks. "Welcome to our school. Our goal is to make you a competent lawman. We hope to teach you how to handle yourself in a gunfight, fistfight, and how to maintain safety during an arrest or a manhunt. To accomplish this, we will hold the following classes:

1. Law. Classroom time to teach you Colorado and Texas county and state laws. Federal duties of a US Marshal will also be included.

2. Hand to hand combat. Field house training in defending yourself while disabling a fist fight.

3. Tracking class. Field and classroom experience on how to use tips in tracking while on a manhunt.

4. Safe setups. You will be presented different scenarios and how to manage them safely. For example, you will be shown the way to make an arrest in a building vs on the trail.

5. Firearms training. This is the most important part of your training. In this world, the gun rules. A lawman needs to master firearms if he wishes to stay alive. We hope to make you competitive gunfighters."

"In closing, remember that outlaws express contempt towards lawmen but law abiding people feel comfort in having you around. You are not in this profession to please outlaws. Do your job ethically but I implore you, never put your lives in danger to save an outlaw. The one line that you will now hear will also be repeated frequently before graduation—WHEN AN OUTLAW DRAWS ON YOU, IT'S KILL OR BE KILLED!"

The next day, the program started. Every day between 8 and 9AM, the law instructor, Cyril Goldbeck, went over the standard statewide laws as well the idiosyncrasies of each county. This was a major challenge to cover two large states. In addition, he covered the Federal Laws of the US Marshal Service to include: serving processes, organizing a trial, protecting judges and prosecutors, transferring prisoners, attending executions and the major one—Federally ordered manhunts.

The tracking instruction was twice a week and lead by a true Native American Cheyenne called Yazzie. His message was that tracking wasn't just following tracks. He insisted that each squad on a manhunt should always follow the man known to be the best tracker of that squad. Every class, he revealed new tips on identifying a track that was unique to the outlaws' horses they were following. Every student was convinced that Yazzie would run out of new pointers before graduation, but that was not the case. They all learned to take the time to study tracks before embarking on the chase. Yazzie's words were truly words of wisdom.

Hand to hand combat was Jake's weakness but it was Willie's domain. The instructor, Quint Abrams, emphasized that it was not a lawman's goal to beat the pulp out of an opponent. The proper goal was self-defense and disabling the opponent. His three major defense strategies were:

1. "Avoid being hit. With an oncoming punch duck down, move sideways, back off and keep moving."
2. "Disable the opponent. Kick him in the groin, poke him in the eye, dislocate his shoulder, break fingers back, clip his knee sideways, and twist your body 360 degrees to kick him in the face. Of course, to learn all these disabling techniques, every student was the guinea pig."

3. "Make contact hits count. Don't punch an opponent in different spots. Choose a sensitive spot, such as the nose or an eye, and repeatedly hit him in the same spot. The pain will compound itself."

4. "If a losing opponent pulls a hidden knife or small pistol, he means to kill you. Don't hesitate, pull out your derringer and shoot him. That's the only solution—'kill or be killed.'"

Commandant Peabody's classes were the most beneficial to the many greenhorns in the class. He covered how to safely arrest outlaws in a saloon, how to enter an outlaw camp, how to detect an ambush site, how to secure your camp to avoid visits from unwanted visitors, how to perform a cabin siege, how to protect a stagecoach, how to equalize odds and so on. Every class he covered two or three scenarios, and like Yazzie, he never ran out of subject matter. Jake told Willie that as much as he had experience as a bounty hunter, he learned something new in all of Peabody's classes.

The firearms instruction by Milo Hapburn were the most important of all classes. A lawman needed to use firearms as an extension of his body and be confident that his guns would save his life if used properly. The class started the season with the fast draw and point shoot with one hand. Students would practice the draw for hours on their own. When live ammo was added, Jake irritated the instructor by demonstrating a clumsy draw and missing 90% of his targets. When it got to rifle training at 100 yards, Jake couldn't hit the barn door or the barn.

Finally, Milo lost control and got in Jake's face in front of the entire class. "What's wrong with you Harrison, no one can be such a klutz. How do you expect to function as a lawman if you can't master the pistol and rifle?"

That is when an observing Commandant stepped forward and said, "Jake, it's time to fess up and give this man and your class a proper demonstration." "Ok sir."

Jake then instructed Willie to place three tin cans at 15 yards and ten more at 100 yards, while he loaded his two guns. With the Commandant holding a stopwatch, he said, "GO."

Jake drew and shot all three cans, but each one shot straight up. As the three cans reached their apogee some 8—10 feet up, Jake shot all three causing the cans to make an acute change in direction. The six shots were one after the other separated by only a few seconds. By then, Milo's lower jaw was down to his chest as Mr. Peabody said, "time 8 seconds."

Not missing a step, he holstered his pistol and grabbed his rifle and shot the ten cans at 100 yards as fast as he could run the rifle's lever. The cans kept falling till he got to the last one which remained on the railing. "Well Jake, you missed one, guess you'd better do some practicing."

Jake knew he had hit the last can, so he spotted it with a 50X binocular. He smiled and said, "take a look Commandant."

Spotting the lone can, the Commandant said, "what, someone tied a wire around it," as Willie was on the ground laughing himself silly.

Milo was flabbergasted and stepped up to

Jakes face, in front of the entire class, as he whispered, "WHY."

The Commandant stepped up and said, "I believe I can answer that. He didn't want to demoralize the class with his firearm prowess. He wanted each student to improve on their own merit."

Milo thought about the situation and yelled out, "from now on Mr. Harrison will be my assistant instructor. If you have half a brain, you'll be lucky to learn from him and some day it will save your life."

Throughout the 100 days of training, Jake and Willie became close friends. Jake spent extra hours training Willie with draw and point shooting. He also introduced him to a sawed-off shotgun in a backpack holster and taught him how to shoot it from the hip. In return, Willie sparred regularly with Jake. Jake refined the techniques of avoiding and disabling his opponent, which Willie insisted was his best defense.

Willie's pastime was reading the three

bounty hunting books by Swanson, Harnell and McWain. In the evenings, while playing cards, they discussed their plans for the future. It was clear all along that Jake would apply to the US Marshal Service. Willie was more motivated by the grandeur and financial benefits of being a bounty hunter. Seeing the road Willie was planning he finally spoke out, "Willie. A bounty hunter has to be faster and smarter than all outlaws. It is also a very dangerous way to make a living, although it's safer if you have a partner."

"Well, I've been poor all my life and I doubt a black man will ever find a partner with a white man, so I'll try it solo for a while. If I can build up a nest egg, I know that I'll eventually apply to the US Marshal Service. Heck, we may even meet up again."

The graduation was held a week before Christmas. Awards were given for the top three spots of each of the five classes. Jake took first place in firearms and scenario setups. Willie won first place in hand combat and, to everyone's surprise, third place in firearms.

As the ceremony was coming to an end, the Commandant got up to hand the "certificates of completion" but hesitated as he added, "over the years I occasionally meet an outstanding individual that is well grounded and secure with his ability, knows it, but doesn't brag or show off. That's a man you want covering your back. This plaque goes to such a man, Jake Harrison." The assembly erupted in applause, whistles, hoots and guffaws, as the entire assembly gave Jake a standing ovation.

For the next ten days, the graduates were allowed to remain in the bunkhouse with meals. This allowed them time to find work and move. Jake had applied to the US Marshal Service in early December and had an appointment with Captain Ennis two days before Christmas.

***

"Welcome to the Marshal Service, Mr. Harrison. I'm Captain Ennis's secretary, Clifton Gibson. Please start filling out some paperwork while the Captain finishes the weekly meeting with his marshals."

Jake start filling out the standard informative forms but was surprised when he saw a form for his last will. It included a space to add beneficiary names, and a list of assets including bank accounts. Fortunately, this last form would have to wait as a group of well healed marshals exited the office and Jake was escorted into the Captain's office. Before leaving, Clifton handed the Captain a file.

"So, you're the famous Jake Harrison, are you aware that someone has been busy getting letters of recommendation on your behalf?"

"No sir, but I can see my dad doing that."

"Well I have letters from lawmen to include: Amos Harrison in Waco, Milton Cassidy in Dallas, Abe Granger in Trinidad, Keith Stratton in Walsenburg, Garrett Galvin in Colorado City, Preston McAllister in Pueblo, Henry Buckland in Colorado Springs, and Joshua Claybourne in Castle Rock. Plus, the new railroad VP N. Duseldorf."

"Oh my, that's a bit embarrassing."

"No son, I believe you earned all this praise. In addition, I have a strong recommendation from Dutton Peabody who recommends you be offered a job in the manhunt squad. That squad is usually reserved for experienced marshals."

"Sir, I would gladly take any position, I'm willing to start at the bottom and work myself up. I'm looking for a long-term career move."

"Well with your recommendations, your Lawman School certificate and your solo bounty hunting experience, I'm ready to offer you a position on a manhunting squad. We have a man retiring and that leaves a spot open. The squad leader is Sargent Byron Ambrose, the long-range expert is Dwight Berwick, the tracker and short-range rifleman is Furman Belcher. You'll be the fast draw gunfighter and expert in jungle warfare. You see, several of your references mention the benefit and safety for the squad's use of jungle paraphernalia."

"I'd be honored to accept this offer and I'll do my best."

"Very good, the pay is $90 a month with housing and meals covered by the Marshal Service. Horses are provided for your use. If you get hurt or sick you have medical coverage with disability income. Whenever your squad brings in outlaws with bounties, the rewards and petty cash are yours to divide amongst yourselves. The Marshal Service gets the horses, firearms and stolen monies in the outlaws' possession. In the event of your death, we need to know who your beneficiaries are to dispose your assets and life insurance. You have unlimited ammo and replacement of damaged or stolen firearms. Basically, you need to supply your clothing and personal items."

"Although we don't have a dress code, most marshals on manhunt squads wear a blue/grey hickory shirt with dark gray pants and a black hat. It helps with camouflage when on the trail."

"You can move into the barracks anytime. Dwight Berwick resides there whereas Byron and Furman live in town with their families. Good luck and stay safe."

Before leaving the office, Jake finished all the forms including his last will and testament. Without delay, Jake said his goodbyes to the instructors and the students left in the bunkhouse. It was bittersweet to lose contact with Willie, but both felt that they would meet again. The next day, Jake moved into the barracks to begin his next journey.

***

CHAPTER 6

US MARSHAL HARRISON

While unpacking, Dwight came over to say hello. "Nice to meet you, we hear some nice things about you. Once you're ready, Byron and Furman are waiting for us at the Captain's office for your swearing in and badge issue. Afterwards we'll go to the range. We'd like to do some friendly shooting while getting to know each other, heh."

Once at the office, Captain Ennis met with the squad in his office. "Before the swearing in, I want to cover some issues not mentioned at the Lawman School. Any US Marshal, whether solo or with a squad, has the right to:

1. Hire some help and or even organize a posse—all legally deputized.
2. Set up an office to bring order in a lawless community.
3. Settle mine uprisings and resolve range wars.
4. Arrest any lawman charged with malfeasance.
5. Travel across state lines to enforce the law and arrest outlaws."

"Just so you are aware, Jake, you are joining a confrontational squad that will often require the use of lethal force with a firearm."

"I understand and I'm happy to serve."

"Very well, according to the Colorado US Marshal statutes, do you Jake Harrison promise. . . . . so help your God?"

"I do."

"Congratulations, and welcome to the service and your squad," as the Captain affixes a Deputy US Marshal badge to Jake's vest. After the applause and handshakes, "now let's all retire to the range. I want to see this expert shooting your references claimed, heh!"

At the range, Byron set the fast draw competition. "On the Captain's order, you and I will draw and shoot at the six cans on the railing at ten yards. The competition ends once someone fires all six rounds."

Captain Ennis yells "GO." Jake drew and shot three cans before Byron got his first shot off. By Jake's sixth round, Byron had hit his first can but missed the second. After the smoke cleared, Captain Ennis said, "I see, Furman let's move to the speed rifle."

Set at forty yards were 20 cans on the railing.. On GO, the shooting began. Jake shot all 10 cans while Furman had three down. "Again, I see. Just for your info, Jake had four spent casings in the air before the first one hit the ground. Well, let's move on to long-range."

Dwight says, "I don't think this squad can tolerate another defeat. Can I just pass?"

"No way, we all need to see what Jake can do."

Dwight relents and says, "At 500 yards is a steel 5-gallon pail. On a rifle rest, we get three shots."

The Captain says, "that's an impossible shot"

Dwight adds, "it's a tough shot, but I usually get one hit out of three."

Jake went first. After adjusting his 8X Malcolm scope and placing his Win 76 on the rifle rest, he took aim and fired three times. Each shot yielded a rolling pail as Dwight was seen unloading his rifle.

Byron looked at Jake and said, "it's clear to me that you are not just a master shootist, but that you are confident and secure with your firearms. Welcome to the squad. Now let's go to work."

***

Captain Ennis explained their first assignment. "I've received word that there is a gang of marauding outlaws terrorizing the ranchers between Colorado Springs and Limon. That's a 70 mile stretch that is beyond Sheriff Henry Buckland's jurisdiction. To make it worse, there is no lawman in the small settlement of Limon, and the railroad is threatening to bypass Limon if the lawlessness is not resolved before their arrival in 1888."

"This four-member gang is unknown to us. They are hitting ranches for their payroll. These ranchers are not close to banks, so they tend to keep a lot of cash in their safes to meet monthly payrolls. They have killed, raped, maimed and tortured the ranchers and their wives. These animals have to be stopped and restitution needs to be made."

Byron asks, "where do we start?"

"Take the train to Colorado Springs and speak to Sheriff Henry Buckland."

The two-hour train ride to cover seventy miles avoided a two-day ride on horseback. Arriving at the depot, Jake went to the stock car to get their horses while the other three guys were talking to the sheriff.

"Are you three the entire squad?'"

Byron says, "no we have one more member, a newbie. Here he comes." Sheriff Buckland turns around and sees an old friend. "Well hello Jake, guess you made it to the Marshal Service, heh?"

"Yes sir, nice to see you again."

"Well sheriff, what is the story?"

"This gang of marauders robbed six ranches coming north from Kit Carson. They managed to kill one rancher and rape one woman. Now they are working their way west from Limon to here. They have already spread their depredations on three ranches. If you head east for the next 70 miles, you'll encounter them. Good luck and don't take any chances, these are killers."

On their way, the squad stopped at every ranch and warned them of the killers coming their way to rob them or worse. The second day they came to a ranch where the owner was being loaded in a wagon to be attended by a doctor to treat his broken arm.

After making certain that some cowhands would stay with the rancher's wife, the squad had to decide how to apprehend them. Byron said, "we have two choices. First, we can watch the next ranch and attack them once they enter. That may put the people in danger to have a gunfight in their home. The second is to track them and enter their camp to make the arrest. Any other ideas?"

Jake added, "there is a third approach. We can go to the next ranch and have the rancher and his wife hide in the bunkhouse with a shotgun. We then can wait for them in the house. One man to receive them, one man as a backup, and two men outside the ranch house to prevent a rear entry in the kitchen."

Furman and Dwight both supported this third alternative. Byron added, "I agree. Furman and Dwight, you position yourselves outside, Jake will meet them as they enter, since this is his idea, and I'll be his backup."

The squad met with Mr. Grossman at the Circle G ranch. The owner was glad to oblige when he heard the story and the squad's plans. "Mister Grossman, if an outlaw comes to the bunkhouse, don't hesitate. Shoot him as he opens the door, you're not going to get another chance."

Around 10AM, horses were heard approaching the ranch house. One rider went straight to the bunkhouse to check on potential witnesses. Byron's last-minute suggestion to Jake, "if the outlaw who busts in has a pistol drawn with a hammer cocked, it's too late to warn him to put his hands up, just shoot him with your sawed-off shotgun."

The events developed quickly. The second man was dispatched to go around the house and enter from the rear door. The leader and one toady stepped on the porch. The leader kicked the front door open and entered as Jake shot him with both barrels. The dead man went flying off the porch and landed in the yard. The other man was frozen in place when he saw Jakes pistol pointing at him. At that moment a shotgun blast was heard at the bunkhouse and Dwight was heard saying, "my man is down, caught my rifle's butt in the face and he dropped like a rock in water."

At the closing, the outlaw's saddle bags were found to be full of money totaling some $22,000. The two dead outlaws were tied to their horses' saddles and the other two were brought alive to Sheriff Buckland. Eventually, all four outlaws were identified and wanted posters were found. The bounties totaled $3,500 which the squad divided equally five ways, leaving a portion for Mr. Grossman. The horses and firearms were sold, and the funds wired to Captain Ennis. The petty cash of $182 was given to Sheriff Buckland for arranging the return of $22,000 to the victims.

As per routine after a caper ended, Byron then sent a telegram to the Captain asking if they should return to Denver or proceed to their next assignment. The answer came back within 15 minutes.

> Proceed to Pueblo by train ASAP STOP
> Go east to Fowler and see Sheriff Edson Adell ASAP STOP
> Cabin siege in progress STOP

***

The squad took the train and covered the 100 miles to Pueblo in three hours. Arriving at noon, they proceeded immediately to Fowler and traveled all night on the well-traveled road, with a full moon. By morning they arrived in Fowler. Sheriff Adell greeted them and explained the situation.

"My deputy, Fletcher Bacon, is watching the cabin with 50X binoculars. You'll find him just five miles east, off the access road to the cabin but he'll clearly be visible from the main road."

"What kind of outlaws are we dealing with?"

"The worst kind, they are kidnappers who put their victims up for ransom but kill them once the ransom is paid. They are cowards, drunks, and real scoundrels that shoot if confronted. The victims' families have put up some hefty rewards, dead or alive. Half of Pueblo is up in arms from their loss."

"Do you have any proof that these are the kidnappers and how many are there?"

"There are six of them, and the proof will be retrieving an incredible amount totaling $35,000 of ransom money. Plus, once you capture them, I'm sure we'll get one to implicate the others if we offer him a reduced sentence.

In this instance, there's one who is not too swift and will likely squeal on the others."

"Why do you say one outlaw is not too swift?" "When was the last time you saw an outlaw riding a 'piebald' horse?"

"Wow, what a way to mark a gang!"

Thirty minutes later, the squad found Deputy Bacon by the access road. The squad tied their horses and spoke to the deputy. Byron asked, "any chance there may be some hostages in the cabin?"

"This cabin belongs to an old recluse. I haven't seen him, so I suspect he's dead."

"Any suggestions how we should proceed?"

"No sir, all I can say is that you can't smoke them out since they cook outside and there is no chimney. Guess that leaves rushing the cabin once they're asleep or find a way to forcefully get them to vacate the cabin."

Byron was receiving suggestions from Furman and Dwight as Jake was quietly listening. Byron finally said, "guess there is no simple safe solution. We'll wait till nightfall and once the talking stops, we'll hope that they drank themselves to sleep. We'll then rush the cabin and shoot anyone who presents a gun in our faces."

Jake saw something in the trees and had an idea. "Sarge, I can empty that cabin and put the outlaws out of commission without a single gunshot!"

"Really, how can you do that?"

"You all turn around, look 25 yards ahead, and see what is dangling from the right side of that big oak tree."

In unison, every man broke out with a huge smile. There hung a 10X14 inch hornet's nest. Furman added, "Harrison, you are one rotten rapscallion. I love it." Dwight added, "I can just see it now, can you imagine waking up to find the cabin full of unhappy hornets?" Byron chimed in, "I'm beginning to like this jungle warfare!"

With Deputy Bacon staying with the horses, at midnight, Jake cautiously covered the sleeping hornet's nest with a burlap bag and cut it off the branch. The squad then walked to the cabin and positioned themselves on the porch. Inside, the outlaws were out and snoring away. Fortunately, the front door was not locked. Byron opened the door as Jake uncovered the nest and wrapped it hard against the door frame to break the nest open. He then threw it in the cabin and closed the door.

A minute later, loud words were coming from the cabin. "What the hell, ouch, ouch, ouch. Jezess, what is that buzzing? I got bugs in my ears and in my hair. Ouch, ouch, ouch damn it. One man yelled out, they're after my thing-y. Hornets, I'm covered with hits, let's get out of here before they kill us."

All six outlaws were trying to get out the door at the same time. Several were trampled in the mayhem. Eventually, they all rolled off the porch and Byron closed the cabin door. The outlaws were rubbing dirt over their faces and bodies. Their bodies were covered with pock marks and welts. The man who was sleeping in "commando" had his manhood swollen into a balloon—it was no longer a tiny thing-y.

The squad was all bent over laughing at the outlaws' antics. Eventually, to make things worse, Furman and Dwight manacled the outlaws with their hands in their backs. Jake added, "hey Furman, who's the rotten rapscallion now. How do you expect them to scratch themselves?"

"Tough. For once these animals are on the receiving end, heh!"

When they arrived in town, the outlaw with the swollen tool was in trouble. The swollen skin was preventing him from peeing. When offered a doctor, if he gave the gang's names, Mr. Commando spewed out their names.

Before leaving town, similar arrangements were carried out. The rewards of $6,000 were shared with the sheriff and his deputies. The recovered loot of $35,000 would be returned to the victims' families. As usual, the sale of horses and firearms was sent to Captain Ennis.

Before leaving Fowler, a telegram from Captain Ennis instructed them to return to Pueblo and take the train west to Salida. There, they would be assigned the responsibility of escorting two prisoners to the Colorado

Territorial prison in Cañon, some 60 miles east of Salida.

***

After a full day's ride to Pueblo, the squad took the train to Salida and arrived four hours later. Arriving at the train depot, a messenger instructed them to proceed to the Federal Courthouse building to meet with Judge Carlisle Bannester and Sheriff Elwin Abbott.

After introductions were made, Judge Bannester started, "The situation is that we have the Burkholder brothers who have been sentenced to hang. These are ruthless killers who had led ten other outlaws on a bank robbing spree throughout western Colorado. The problem is that the bulk of the gang is still free and have promised to free their bosses before they are hung—at any cost."

Byron interrupts the judge and says, "I don't see a problem, lets hang them now."

The head of the town council spoke up. "The gang has promised to burn the town down if we do that. That also means that many town folks will also die in the melee. For that reason, we want these two out of here and on their way to the Colorado Territorial Prison in Cañon, Colorado. Furman adds, "so, put them on the train in a prison car made for this type of transfer."

The railroad executive spoke up. "This gang has been known to blow up tracks that causes dangerous and expensive derailments. The gang has promised such activity if we transfer them by train. It is too dangerous to expect our customers to be exposed to such dangers when we know the derailment will happen."

Dwight spoke up, "so you think it's ok to risk the life of four US Marshals just to get your bidding done?"

The councilman and railroad man were both clamoring in their defense. "Enough," shouted Byron. "It's our job and we'll do it. Get your prisoners in manacles and we'll pick them up after we get some dinner and buy supplies for the trip. Let it be well known that we are taking these two guilty and sentenced outlaws to Salida by the main road and not cross-country."

While the squad was having a late dinner, the train departed for Salida without the Burkholder brothers. Later, the scout had witnessed the US Marshals picking up their bosses, and securing them to horses by a neck collar chained to a stirrup.

> Meanwhile, some five miles from Salida, the Burkholder gang was talking to their scout. "I saw them secure the bosses to their horse and casually walked their horses out of town." The current leader, Sonny, said, "I can't believe they would be so stupid to travel the open road. If that is the case, let's take the advantage and set up an ambush before nightfall."

Back on the trail, the squad was leading their charge by traveling cross-country. Byron explained, "I'm sure the gang is now setting an ambush on the main road, so we'll have uninterrupted traveling till nightfall. The tradeoff may mean a camp attack tonight, but by using Jake's jungle tools, we'll do alright."

When darkness arrived, it was totally dark on a moonless night. As they arrived at a stream with trees and good grass, the squad set up camp. After cooking themselves a meal of bacon, eggs, beans, biscuits and coffee, the prisoners demanded water and some dinner. Byron stepped up to them and applied a muzzle. "Shut up and we'll treat you only like animals as you are. You don't demand, you don't ask, and you don't get a thing from us. If you poop or pee in your pants, too bad, we aren't cleaning you up."

Jake then proceeded to set up a safe camp. The first thing he did was to blindfold the prisoners but leave them close to the fire so they can be seen by their gang. He then placed a cord six inches off the ground and kept it taught between trees all around the campsite. Tin cans were tied to a secondary string over a branch. Anyone tripping on the string would ring the clump of tin cans. For good measure, Jake added three bear traps and several board anchored nails throughout the back of the camp in case of a rear approach. Dwight asked, "how do you know that an approaching outlaw will take the path where your boobytraps are set."

"In total darkness, man like an animal will always take the path of least resistance, and that's the path that is loaded with goodies, heh?" For the last part of the safe camp, the bedrolls were stuffed with twigs and grass and a cowboy hat left at the head to look like a man asleep in his bedroll. Meanwhile, the squad had their faces smeared with charcoal to camouflage themselves. They were then set up sitting behind large trees to blend in—and of course each man armed with a double barrel shotgun with #3 Buckshot—the ideal Buckshot for nighttime use. Finally, with a roaring campfire to be sure the outlaws found them, they waited for their prey.

> Meanwhile, at the ambush site, nothing was happening. Sonny finally said, "it's two hours past sundown and they aren't here yet.

Those bastards are moving cross-country. Let's mount up and go find their camp. We'll shoot them in their bedrolls."

Several hours later the campfire was finally detected. Leaving their horses tied to tree branches, they walked some 300 yards towards the fire. Within 100 yards of the camp, Sonny whispered, "you three men go around and enter the camp from the rear and flanks. We'll give you plenty of time to get in position, just whistle when you're ready."

Sonny and his six men waited as they came within 25 yards of the campfire. What they didn't know was that Jake had seen them and knew that some men had been sent around. Jake waited but one of Sonny's men decided to get closer as he triggered the cord and rattled the secondary cord that jingled the tin cans. The remainder of the squad became awake as the stillness of the night had been curtailed.

A loud snap was heard followed by a howl from hell. At the same time on the camp's opposite side several loud squeals of pain were heard as men stepped on boarded nails. Sonny responded to his men's screams by yelling to the others, "shoot them in their bedrolls, now!"

The flashes from seven pistols revealed the outlaws' locations. The squad let go both barrels and the eight Buckshot loads wiped out the entire seven killers. After verifying that they were all dead, it became clear that Byron had been hit with a round in his gun-hand shoulder. Before attending to his wound, the squad went to tend to the outlaws stuck in Jake's traps. It took two men to reopen the beartrap and Jake volunteered to pull out the jagged nails. The nails came out hard and with violent screaming from the maimed recipients.

Jake then attended to Byron wound. The entrance wound was cleansed, sterilized with carbolic acid and probed with forceps. There was no exit wound and the bullet could not be pulled out of the shoulder's joint. "Sorry Byron, but you need to have this bullet surgically removed. You need to go back to Salida."

After bandaging the three outlaws, the squad had to decide what to do with the dead and injured outlaws as well as Byron. While discussing the different options, Jake kept quiet since he was the newbie. It was Furman who made the best and final suggestion. "Byron is going back to Salida for medical care. I'm going with him to lead the seven horses with dead men and the three live outlaws. We're only ten miles from Salida and we'll make it in 1 1/2 hour. As soon as I take care of business with Sheriff Abbott, I'll rush back here where you'll be waiting for me."

Three hours later, Furman made it back. The squad then moved to the main road and made it back to Cañon the next day without any further attacks or interruptions. With the prisoners delivered, Furman sent the usual telegram to Captain Ennis and did inform him of Byron's mishap. The message came back"

Have Byron return to Denver by train STOP
Proceed to Pueble ASAP STOP
Sheriff Mcallister needs help STOP

After assisting him, return to Denver for meeting STOP

***

Two hours later, they walked into Sheriff McCallister's office. Furman asks, "what is the problem and how may we help you?"

"For the past three days, a gang of animals have commandeered the west side of town. They have taken over Murphy's bar and have been terrorizing the merchants in this neighborhood. So far, they killed four innocent bystanders during a drunken shooting spree, robbed four merchants and raped one lady after beating her to a pulp. They have beaten Sam Murphy into submission. These men are psychopaths with no remorse or care for human life and have turned part of this town into a lawless haven. It's just a matter of time before they rob our bank which is expected to receive payroll funds for several mines. If we don't stop them many more innocent people will die."

Jake asked, "how many are there and where are they today?"

"There are six and we can find them at Murphy's."

Furman responded, "you all get your shotguns and we'll go collect those miscreants. While setting up a mode of operation, Jake suggestion had the most support. Deputy Cavill guards the rear door, Sheriff McCallister guards the front door as Jake, Furman and Dwight rush the front door with shotguns.

Looking over the batwing doors, Jake confirmed where the outlaws were seated. On signal, the trio of US Marshals rushed the saloon. Jake was chosen to walk right up to the gang as Furman and Dwight were backup with their shotguns at port arms.

Jake worked quickly; he slammed his shotgun butt on the back of the first man's head as he then swung the shotgun's barrels onto the side of the outlaw to his right. He then said, "you four, keep both hands on the table." One man already had his hand on his pistol and pulled the pistol out to shoot Jake. Jake simply pulled the trigger and shot him point blank with his sawed-off shotgun. The outlaw rocked backwards in his chair and went head over heels as the chair's back hit the floor. After that, all hands went up and were manacled behind their backs. As they were walking the outlaws to jail, Dwight said, "Je-eez, you stink more than a dead animal. What have you been doing, washing in a spittoon?"

"It don't matter," says the sheriff. "They'll go to the gallows smelling like the animals they are."

With financial arrangements settled, Sheriff McCallister would send bounty rewards to Jake's account, horses and firearms to Captain Ennis and the petty cash of $271 to the sheriff for his handling of the funds and sales.

**

Arriving in Denver, the trio proceeded to the Captain's office. Furman and Dwight were invited into the office first, and after some time, Jake was then asked to join them.

Inside the office, there was another man next to the Captain. The Captain started. Byron has decided to retire since his injury to his gun-hand will be a permanent disability. I don't like to see a three-man squad, so I'm adding a fourth man. This is Deputy Dalton Barker. He has ten years' experience with the service and his specialty is shotgun shooting from the hip. This is keeping with the service's trend of using shotguns to intimidate outlaws into submission."

"Now the second issue is to name a squad leader. Jake, both Furman and Dwight feel comfortable working with you. They both feel you are a man exhibiting quiet confidence and sound judgement. They are both waiving their right to become the squad leader and request that you take the lead. Do you accept the position?"

"Yes, I'm comfortable with the challenge."

"Very good, so with the paygrade change comes the rank change to Sargent and a full-fledged US Marshal status and badge. Congratulation young man."

"Now for your next assignment. Good news, you all get a three- day 'R & R' in Denver. Come and see me in three days, heh."

That evening the two single men, Dwight

and Dalton, decided to celebrate Jake's new status. They invited him to the "Lucky 10 of Clubs" for drinks and a friendly card game. As they had a game going, two ruffians came to their table and accosted them. "We don't like lawmen in our saloon. We want you to leave before you regret coming here."

Jake spoke up, "gentlemen, it's obvious you are brewing for a fight. Let's take it outside and I'll take on the best of you two without guns or badges."

The man who was not talking started to smile. Jake noticed that he was built like a gorilla with a bent over body and arms that were too big to hang to his side.

As they stepped outside, the bar patrons followed them and formed a spectator circle in the street.

The fight starts. Gorilla Man produces three punches which Jake ducked and swerved aside. Jake's first attack was a powerful kick to Gorilla Man's groin. The kick lifted the burly man off his feet and was associated with a loud groan. As he was still bent over holding his crotch, Jake pumped three quick punches to the man's right eye.

Gorilla man responded like a grizzly who had been awaken by a kick. He looked like he wanted to eat Jake alive. Without planning, he rushed Jake as Jake stepped sideways but caught his right arm and forced it backwards and up—loudly dislocating his right shoulder out of its socket with a pop. That also angered his opponent even more and Gorilla Man made one final charge at Jake. Jake did a 360-degree spin and slammed his right foot into Gorilla Man's knee—a sideways clip. The damage lead to another pop as the leg angled sideways in a strange angle.

Gorilla Man couldn't take a step forward, so he grabbed Jake in a bearhug. Feeling like in a vice, Jake bit the man's ear and amputated half the ear off. Jake realized he had humiliated the man and knew that the worse was about to happen. True to form, Gorilla Man pulled a long knife out of his boot and was coming to gut Jake alive. Jake had anticipated the move and pulled his 41-caliber derringer out of his vest pocket and quickly shot Gorilla Man in the foot.

"Hey man, you've pushed the envelope. Now you have to choose. Drop the knife and go to jail with some medical help. You would only be charged with assaulting a US Marshal, or, you come at me and the second shot will be in your brain. Your choice."

Minutes passed and Gorilla Man finally said, "I'm done."

***

Two days later the squad met with the Captain.

"We have a situation in Amarillo, Texas. Judge Harland Hobart, a Federal Judge, was sent to settle a range war. At the inquiry's conclusion, the judge ruled against the rancher, Hiram Brewster, and charged him $5,000 in fines for destroying barbwire fences and stampeding cattle to ruin homesteader crops."

"A week later, Brewster went on a rampage and ordered his regulators to attack three neighboring homesteaders. Unfortunately, three homesteaders were killed. In response,

Sheriff Earle Gusfield organized a 15-man posse and went to Brewster's ranch and arrested him."

"Today, eight of Brewster's regulators have kidnapped the judge and are holding him in the town's house for dignitaries. If Brewster is not released in the next three days, the judge will be killed. Your job is to free the judge and keep him alive—at all costs. Federal judges cannot be held hostage or threatened. Otherwise, the system falls apart."

That night the squad took the overnight express train to Amarillo some 400 miles thru Colorado and New Mexico. Arriving in the morning, the squad had breakfast with Sheriff Gusfield in Ernie's Diner. Jake asked, "Any idea how we can get the judge out in one peace?"

"Judge Hobart is being kept a prisoner in a fortress by eight well known violent gunfighters. The only way to save the judge is either to release Brewster or kill the eight regulators."

Jake answered, "I agree, we'll go free the judge if you and your deputy are willing to guard the front and rear door in case some regulators try to escape. We need to send the message that we don't tolerate judicial tampering."

Fully loaded with 00 Buckshot, the four Marshals entered the house. Teams of two men started clearing each room. One man would enter and fall to his knees as the other would stand at the door ready to back up the entry man. There was no discussion and demand to raise hands. When a regulator was found, either marshal would fire at him with his shotgun. On the first floor, four regulators were sequentially eliminated from rooms or hallways.

Arriving on the second floor, at the top of the staircase was a regulator who started shooting at Jake as Dalton cut him down before he made contact with any of the marshals. The next regulator was found guarding a door and started shooting at the US Marshals. The marshals fired back with shotguns and literally pulverized the regulator. After clearing the rooms, it was clear that the last two regulators were with Judge Hobart in the only room that wasn't cleared.

Jake knocked at the door and even asked if he could come in. When invited in, he left his shotgun and entered wearing his Colt as his only firearm. One regulator was holding a pistol to the judge's head while the other was pointing his pistol at Jake. Both of the regulator's hammers were not pulled back.

Jake spoke first, "you have six dead men and I have three marshals outside. You are not escaping even if you kill the judge." Jake sees the judge's eyes bug out in shock. "The only way for you to live is to give up since your battle is lost. What do you say?"

A minute escapes as the regulator holding his gun at the judge starts to lower his pistol. The other regulator said, "we're dead men either way, so go to hell. Jake saw the regulator's eyes blink as his thumb moved to pull the hammer back. That is when Jake drew his pistol and shot both regulators in the face—dropping them both to the floor like a poleaxed beef. Judge Hobart was shuddering in his seat and finally said, "officer, you saved my life, if ever I can do something for you, please don't hesitate to ask. Now, if you'll excuse me, I have to change my pants, heh."

After making contact with Captain Ennis with the good news, the squad was ordered back to Denver for a very important development. Little did Jake realize that this development would change the course of his life forever.

***

BOOK TWO

---◆---

HANNAH

CHAPTER 7

MEETING HANNAH

Stepping in the Captain's office, Mr. Gibson asked Jake to enter first as the remainder of the squad was asked to have a seat in the waiting room. Jake noticed that Clifton Gibson was wearing a US Deputy Marshal badge. "Did I miss your badge in the past?"

"No sir, I have taken the Lawman School's course and since my graduation, I took the oath for the Marshal Service. So now, the Captain has a lawyer on his marshal's staff."

"Well, congratulation. Welcome aboard!"

Captain Ennis greeted Jake, "I'm glad you're here. First let me thank you for the job you did saving Judge Hobart. The message has gotten around that the Marshal Service protects our Federal judges. You may not know but Judge Hobart travels all thru Colorado and Texas and has requested that you to be assigned to his attachment year-round. For your information, that is never going to happen. Now for the reason you were summoned here today, and this is part of the job I detest."

"I'm sorry to say that I have some very bad news. I've just received a telegram from your dad. Jake, your sister and her husband are dead!"

"What? With a look of shock and disbelief Jake asked, what happened?"

"They were murdered, shot dead."

Jake remained silent. "Concurrently, I received a long letter from a Deputy Sheriff Herb Bixby in New Braunfels, cosigned by a district Judge Hoyt Aiken. They are informing me that George and Rose Sanders had been murdered. To complicate matters, Sheriff Omer Banfield did not investigate the matter and shoved the event under the carpet. This deputy and judge are strongly suggesting that the sheriff is guilty of malfeasance and they want some guidance or help dealing with the matter."

"I've heard that name, Banfield. My dad's replacement when I left to go bounty hunting was a Steve Bochart who had left New Braunfels for the same reason—a crooked sheriff."

"There is more. It appears that there is a large rancher by the name of Hans Klaus that has been coercing your sister's neighbors into selling their homesteads and ranches at reduced values. With you family's demise, the neighbors are afraid for their lives—fear has a way of pushing people to make hasty decisions."

"My last bit of information is that your dad informed me that your sister and brother-in-law have named you as sole beneficiary of their ranch, hundreds of cattle, fifteen horses, agricultural implements, three sections of prime land and all miscellaneous items on the property"

Jake was seen woolgathering in a trance. Captain Ennis waited for Jake to respond.

"Captain, would you consider sending me to New Braunfels to bring this tyrant to justice, arrest the sheriff and whomever else is under Klaus' control?"

Captain did not hesitate, "it so happens that I'm legally bound and have to respond to Deputy Bixby and Judge Aiken in the positive. Yes, I would be honored to send you as a special agent to resolve the mess. Do you wish to have the assistance of one of your squad's members?"

"No, I don't want to leave you short. I'm sure that Deputy Bixby will be of help and I can always deputize another, as is my right to do so as a US Marshal."

"Is there anything else I should know?"

"Yes, the letter also infers that there are many robberies of travelers on the road between New Braunfels and Austin. This is a 50-mile stretch but the majority of waylaying is occurring within 10 miles of New Braunfels. It is also sad to add that two homesteaders were killed during the robberies. I wonder if this is not Klaus' doing, to traumatize the local homesteaders and ranchers, since the robbers are riding horses with the 'Circle K' brand—Klaus' brand."

"Done, I'll be on my way today. It will take

a couple days to cover the 950 miles to New Braunfels by train. I'll keep you posted."

"Good luck, stay safe and come back to me after settling the issues. I'm not proud to say, I hope you sell your ranch and return to us to continue your career as a US Marshal. Again, I extend my sympathies for your loss. Goodbye."

***

Jake gathered his clothes, firearms, jungle warfare saddlebags and his horse. He got a one-way passenger ticket for himself and a tag for his horse in the stock car—paid for with a $40 chit from the US Marshal Service. The first leg of the trip was one way to Amarillo Texas. There he took a room at a local hotel while his horse was kept in the railroad yard's livery. The trip's second leg was direct to New Braunfels. Arriving at noon, Jake had the choice of confronting Sheriff Banfield vs taking a ride two miles east to his sister's ranch. Realizing that there would be ample opportunities to take care of the sheriff, Jake headed to his new home.

The first homestead he came onto was a

small cabin, barn and large chicken coop. He saw someone looking in the window but decided not to stop yet. He continued riding and came onto several homesteads. This time he stopped at each one because they all looked abandoned. To his surprise the homesteads and barns were truly abandoned. Continuing on, he arrived at the Double S ranch. Stepping down, Jake was greeted by a white-haired cowhand.

"Hello Marshal, what brings you here?"

"My name is Jake Harrison. I'm the late Rose Sanders' brother and heir to this ranch. Whom might you be, sir?"

"I'm the ranch foreman, Clayton Briggs, and I'm glad to meet the new owner."

"Fine, walk with me and hopefully you can answer some pressing questions."

Standing in the ranch's parlor, Clayton said, "this is where we found George and Rose. George had been shot in the back and Rose in the head—execution style."

"Did you have the sheriff come and investigate?"

"Yes, he came with the undertaker and took

the bodies away. He only asked me if there were any witnesses. When I said that the cook was in town getting vittles and the cowhands were all on the range, he turned around and walked away. When he was back on his horse, I pressed him and asked what he expected us to do. He answered to continue working the ranch until the new owners were announced and then turned and rode away."

"So, you and how many men stayed on?"

"The cook and nine cowhands."

"How much back pay are you owed."

"One month, $400 would cover it."

Jake pulls out $600 in cash and hands it to Clayton. "Is everyone willing to stay on for now?"

"Yes sir, I'm certain of it."

"Good, here's another $1,200 in two bank drafts. I transferred a large amount from my Denver account to your Ranchers Bank in New Braunfels. Would you keep everything the same for now?"

"Yes, I'd be glad to."

"I've visited my sister only once, so I know

the lay of the land. What I don't know is how many head of cattle I have and what is that second barn for?"

"After the spring roundup, we counted 976 head of cattle and 20 fine riding and cattle cutting horses. There are also several harnessed horses to handle wagons etc. That extra barn is a shed that holds the agricultural implements and some hay. We harvest 300 acres of hay to supplement the herd and horses during winter months. The Sanders were progressive, heck, we even have a baler to process the hay."

"Ok, I'll be back. The next time I'm in town, I'll open accounts in the mercantile and hardware store so you can pick up whatever you need on the ranch."

"That's great, the mercantile we use is Wolfgang's and the hardware/feed store is Heinz's."

For now, I need to find my family's killers. To make my job, would you not mention to anyone that I'm a US Marshal"

"Certainly Mr. Harrison."

"That's Jake, Mr. Harrison was my dad!"

"And I'm Clayton."

After stepping up on his horse, Jake asked, "any idea who might have killed my family?"

"All I know is what George told me, which is that Hans Klaus was pushing hard to buy them out. Klaus also has a bad reputation of abusing your neighbors. It's interesting that your ranch and the Bauer homestead are the only land he has not managed to buy within ten miles of town. I may add that Klaus is still pushing, he has recently offered to double all our wages if we abandon this ranch and move over to his employ. The Sanders were good to us, and none of us are moving."

"Faithful help is hard to find, make sure you add $20 to every man's monthly wages from now on. You have enough funds to start that today."

"But that's not necessary Jake."

"I know, but I want to, and trust me, I can afford it."

"Well I and my men thank you."

"The Bauer homestead is where?"

"It was the first place you passed out of

town, the one with the small cabin and the huge chicken coop—the owner is called the 'egg lady.'"

"Ok, I also passed a huge stream across the road. Does that ever pass thru my land?"

"Yes, thru the entire 2,000 acres you own. That's what makes your land so valuable."

As he was riding away, he turned his horse and asked Clayton, "how do your men unload the manure in the fields?

"Two men load and unload it in a wagon with pitchforks."

"Thanks, see you in a few days."

***

Jake started riding back and when he went over the stream, he decided to follow it along the road. When he came to a large blowdown in the stream, he saw a large pool. Without hesitation, he stopped, undressed and dove in the pool. After a refreshing swim, he stepped out and dressed. As he was putting his gun-belt back on he saw a man in overalls and an old deformed hat arrive at a run. The man took his hat off and Jake was mystified at the unusual medium length blonde hair and blue eyes. The confusion was cleared when the man released his front straps and two fully formed breasts fell out.

Jake scooted down to hide behind the blowdown as the overalls fell to the ground exposing the remainder of her female attributes in a full-frontal view. Jake was wondering if he should announce himself or just sneak away to give this gal some privacy. The lady jumped in the water and Jake decided that this was the best time to skedaddle. Before he could react, he heard whistling and hollering. As three men arrived, one man said, "I told you that was her running from the cabin." The other man added, "let's get down to our union suits and grab her."

The three men threw the gal's overalls and boots in the stream and then quickly ran in the water and grabbed the woman. She fought hard and scratched two of the men's faces. Yet they grabbed both arms and dragged her out of the water, kicking and screaming. Two men straddled her across a large rock and each man held her arms and spread her legs apart. The third man was unbuttoning his suit and it was clear what he was going to do. The gal screamed "no, no, nooh."

Jake knew the "die was cast" and he had to put an end to the vile activities. He hunched down and crept behind the standing man. With his suit's back door open, Jake grabbed his sac and crushed the contents as hard as he could. The miscreant's body flexed and collapsed on his knees as he proceeded to lose his lunch. Jake drew his Colt and yelled to the other men, "let her go or I'm going to shoot off your manhood."

The gal pulled away as Jake said, "Ma'am find a shirt, pants and boots that fit you and get dressed. After she was dressed, Jake added, "now throw the remainder of their clothes and boots in the drink. Afterwards, bring my horse up and take the manacles out of my saddlebags."

"You animals. Get on your bellies and put your hands behind your back. You're going to jail."

"Hey mister, there's no harm done, let us go if you know what's best for you. We work for a powerful man who will kill you if you bring us in."

"Shut up and walk up to your horses."

"Ma'am, please hook the three gun-belts to my saddle horn and walk my horse along."

Once they arrived at the cabin, Jake helped the would-be rapists onto their horses, secured the reins to the railing, and added a second manacle to their ankle as he secured the other end to the stirrup. "Now you turds wait, if you escape, I'll run you down and beat you to a pulp."

Jake then took his saddlebags and walked the gal to the cabin. "Ma'am, not to get personal, but you look like you haven't eaten in days. Here is a can of peaches, some biscuits, and coffee to hold you till I return. Sear and braise this piece of beef and add those vegetables on the counter. Start cooking a stew and when I come back with some flour, we'll make some gravy and have supper, heh."

The gal spoke for the first time, "my name is Hannah, not Ma'am. Do you have to go, I'm afraid the attackers' friends will come looking for them."

"I have to bring these evil men to jail and we'll go back tomorrow to fill out a legal complaint. Until I return, use that shotgun on the wall and shoot anyone threatening you."

"I don't have any shotgun shells."

"Here's a box of OO Buckshot."

"What if they rush the cabin door and I don't have time to get to it?"

"In that case, wear this belted holster with a Colt."

"The Colt is too large for my spindly hands. I was use to shooting my mom's mini pistol, which disappeared during the accident."

Jake took the Colt back and handed her his own 44 Bulldog.

After Hannah got comfortable dry firing it, he loaded the pistol and asked Hannah to fire it. As they stepped on the porch, Jake yells to the manacled men, "watch here, this is what you'll meet if you ever attack this lady again." Hannah fired the Bulldog's five rounds at a nearby stump and finished with a smile.

"Keep this pistol loaded and always wear it.

It's only going to save you if it's available when you need it."

"Before I leave, may I walk around to see what you are missing."

"Yes, but I can't afford anything."

"Not to worry, it won't cost you a penny. You are a victim and I help victims." Jake walked around and wrote items down as he checked the larder, kitchen cabinets, bedroom dressers and two closets. When done taking an inventory he asked, "do you know your attackers?"

"I don't know them by name, but I know they are regulators for Hans Klaus, and their horses' brand of Circle K, fits as well."

As he was about to leave Hannah was fidgeting and finally asked, "are you going to be gone long?"

"It's midafternoon and I'll be back before dark."

"Do you promise as her lips quivered."

"Hannah, I guarantee it. I suspect there are many other issues that make you so afraid, and we'll talk about them later. And by the way, as he opens his vest, I'm US Marshal Jake Harrison, please call me Jake."

"Pleasure to meet you Jake, even if I was not in my best attire." Hannah stepped forward and gave him a kiss on the cheek and added, "and thank you for saving my maidenhood."

***

When Jake arrived in town, he stopped at the Wolfgang Mercantile and met Herman and Helga. After complete introductions, Jake asked if they would fill out his list and would be back in a half hour to pay. He also asked Mrs. Wolfgang to find the listed female clothes to fit Hannah Bauer. Helga simply smiled and said she would be pleased to do so.

After Jake left, Herman read the list out loud: "2 pounds of Arbuckle Ariosa coffee and salt. 5 pounds of flour, large slab of bacon, 10 pounds of beans, baking powder, cheese, crackers, large beef and pork roast, 4 large beefsteaks, canned peaches and a fresh bread with butter if possible. Lady's riding pants/blouse, dresses, work pants and shirts, rain slicker and winter coat, pair of shoes and cowboy boots, cowboy hat, nightgown and female undies but no overalls. Shampoo, smelling soaps, toothbrush, tooth powder, hairbrush, hand mirror, lip color, rouge, a set of sheets and a wool blanket. Privacy papers and those female hygiene products. Three boxes of 44 rimfire, box of #2 and #6 birdshot shotgun shells. One gallon of kerosene, candles and matches. At the end he read, and anything you think Miss Bauer needs."

Jake's next stop was Sheriff Banfield's office. Arriving, he pushed the door open and walked in the three men in their union suits. The sheriff got up and said, "what is the meaning of this? These are Klaus' men and you can't put them in jail."

"Sheriff, I'm a US Marshal and I just caught these men in the act of attempting to rape Hannah Bauer. Keep them in jail and Miss Bauer and I will be back tomorrow to file an official complaint. In addition, I'm also the late Rose Sanders' brother and beneficiary to her farm. Tomorrow, I will review your investigation's report on their murder as well as the reports of the homesteaders killed within ten miles of town."

Sheriff Banfield yelled out, "how dare you, you have no rights in Texas!"

"Wrong, I was sent here at the request of your own District Judge Hoyt Aiken, and I will remain here as the head lawman until I find out who killed my sister and several of your homesteaders."

As Jake was leaving, he saw the deputy smiling as he pushed the prisoners in the cells. Jake walked out as the sheriff was still sputtering in the background.

Before getting back to the mercantile, Jake brought the prisoners' horses to Frank Werner's livery. "Howdy Marshal, what can I do for you."

"These three horses have been confiscated by the US Marshal Service and are for sale."

"Sorry, I can't buy them because they carry the Circle K brand. They will be claimed by Klaus within 24 hours and I'll have no choice but to let them go or suffer the consequences. Now with a court order from Judge Aiken, that would be a different matter."

"I understand and I'll be back with one."

Getting back to the Wolfgang Mercantile, Jake saw four large burlap bags on the counter. Helga greeted him and said, "meat comes from the butcher, Otto Mueller, and I went to get your order. I also added two items, a lady in a dress needs a reticule and a Sunday hat. I think she will like the clothes I've selected, it's the best quality and colors we have."

"Thank you. Now, assuming my order is in these four bags, what is the total cost I owe?"

"$71.12 will cover it."

Jake hands him a bank draft. "Now how much does Miss Bauer owe you on credit?"

"Hannah is like a daughter. I don't carry her in my books. I give her what she needs and pretend to put it in a ledger. She is very frugal, and her needs always border on survival." Helga adds, "you obviously noticed how skinny she is. I cannot believe she lives on the income she gets from selling eggs. We pay her 20 cents a dozen and she brings us 5-dozen a week—that's $1 a week to live on, heh."

"I see, so how much to pay up her account?"

"Well, if you insist, $10 will do it."

"Sure, so here are three $20 double eagles. In addition, I would like to start a credit account for her. Here is a bank draft for $200."?"

"More than generous. Here is the credit booklet. Hannah's purchases will be entered in her book and I initial all purchases."

Helga added, "It appears that you are taking some responsibility for Hannah, which pleases me, but would you explain why and why a US Marshal is in town?"

"Fair enough, I'm the late Rose Sanders' brother and I have become the new owner of their ranch. I recently met Miss Bauer and thwarted a personal attack on her maidenhood. I am a sucker for victims and money is not an issue. You're correct, I will be supporting this young lady. Also, here is a bank voucher of $500 to open an account for my ranch to be used by the foreman, Clayton Briggs, or any of his authorized cowhands."

Herman looked at Jake and asked, "any other reason why you're here?"

"You're very perceptive, sir. I'm officially

here on assignment. I will find out who killed my family and who is waylaying, killing and scaring homesteaders to abandon their farms."

Helga added, "officer, you are up against a concrete wall and your life is in danger. Hannah is also in danger since her land and yours are the only landowners that have refused to sell to Hans Klaus. He will kill you just like he did to your sister and brother-in-law."

"Thank you for your concern, but I assure you that I will bring this ogre down. No man has the right to terrorize his fellow man. I will not stop till justice is reached, and that means Klaus will be held accountable for his depredations."

"Good luck, and bring Hannah to visit, we miss her."

Jake then tied two bags together and dropped two bags behind the saddle's cantle and two bags over the saddle's horn, stepped in the saddle and returned to the Bauer homestead.

***

Once he was riding out of town, he realized what Helga said, that Hannah's life was in danger. Jake promised himself that he would not leave her without protection until the Klaus caper was resolved. Jake found himself pushing his horse to get back, not realizing whether it was to protect her or just wanting to be with her.

Meanwhile, Hannah had tried to keep busy while Jake was gone. She prepared the meat and vegetables and set the stew to slow cook. She even soaked beans for tomorrow. She cleaned her Bulldog and her shotgun. Went to feed and water her horse and chickens. Did some house cleaning, shampooed her hair using an egg concoction, and when she ran out of jobs, tried to read one of her books, but to no avail. Eventually, she went and sat on the porch with her loaded shotgun on her lap. The one thing Hannah promised herself, whether Jake did or did not return, was that she would never let any man abuse or threaten her life and maidenhood again. What she really wanted was to live again as a family when her parents lived. Suddenly, Jake was seen coming down the road and Hannah got the willies—the kind you get when you want everything to go well.

Realizing that darkness was soon upon him, he was pleased to arrive within visibility of the cabin. He relaxed when he saw Hannah sitting on the porch with a double barrel shotgun on her lap and no evidence of visitors.

"Hello the cabin, may I light down?"

With a big smile, "certainly, welcome back during daylight, you're a man of your words."

Jake stepped down, tied the reins to the railing, grabbed two bags and walked up to the porch. Leaving the two bags on the porch, he went back to get the other two bags. Stepping inside, he opened the first bag to expose the vittles he had purchased. Hannah was amazed and said, "I haven't seen so much food since my parents passed away."

The second bag had the miscellaneous items from kerosene to shotgun shells. Hannah asked what the shotgun shells were for.

"The #2 birdshot is for coyotes; the #4 birdshot is for pheasant and rabbits. The 00 Buckshot I gave you was for men but is also good to harvest deer and put down large predators."

The third bag was female clothes. Jake

admitted that Helga had chosen everything. Hannah looked and touched every piece. The smile on her face was constant. One item was wrapped in paper. As Hannah opened it she said, "oops, female undies."

The last bag brought a tear to Hannah's eyes. The personal care items were overwhelming to her. Hannah spotted another package wrapped in paper. This time she peeled back an end to reveal those personal care items with a hoosier belt. When Jake asked what was in the package, Hanna answered, "Never mind."

Hannah could not stop the tears. Jake saw her dismay and said, "Hannah, life doesn't mean that you have to eat all your meals out of a tin plate and a spoon. There is more to life and some luxuries make days more pleasant. You're going to have to dry up those tears, because you are overdue, and I plan to bring you more of these tear-jerking luxuries."

"How can I repay you or even thank you?"

"Simple, go in your bedroom and put on a dress and get gussied up. I'll make coffee and gravy and when you've changed, we'll have supper. I want to know everything about you, and I want us to get to know each other."

Jake had the coffee boiling and the gravy was made and added to the braising stew. The bedroom door opened, and Hannah stepped out. Jake knew he looked foolish with his jaw drooping and his eyes bugged out. Somehow, he heard himself say, "Good God you're beautiful!"

"Oh Jake, you're way too kind, I'm a hayseed, a simple skinny bean pole with bumps along the way. You of all people should know."

"Ma'am, the only thing I will say on that matter is two things. One, beauty is always in the eyes of the beholder—and I'm the beholder. Two, I know there is more to you than a nude body. I feel you are a woman of substance. That's all I'll say for now, except let's eat.

Hannah started to eat and couldn't stop moaning on every morsel. Jake finally asked, "when did you eat last?"

"Two eggs yesterday. That can of peaches you left was gone before you got in the saddle."

As they were eating, Jake was sneaking pieces of beef into Hannah's plate. One time, Hannah caught him and speared his piece of beef thinking he was stealing from her plate. With both forks on the meat, they both started laughing. Hannah, asked, "who's stealing from who?"

"Hannah, if I have anything to say about this, you'll never feel on the edge of starving, ever again."

After the beef stew, they shared a can of peaches and several cups of coffee. Jake started, "who are you Miss Bauer and why are you living here alone?"

"My parents lived in Germany in the 1840's and finally left in 1850 because of religious persecution. My father was a Calvinist, but my mother was Jewish. Because of my mother, my dad was bypassed and eventually lost his job teaching English Literature. They came to this country with enough funds to buy one full section of land and build this cabin, barn and chicken coop.

"My mother had me late in life and I was her only child. Because she felt that God 'favored' her with a child, she named me Hannah which in Hebrew means 'favor.' Throughout my eighteen years, we lived well and had over 200 chickens. We were making $5 a week with eggs and as much selling fresh fowl to Otto Mueller. Everything changed a year ago when Klaus started buying out homesteaders."

"One day Klaus came to see my father and made him a lowball offer to sell him our home. My dad refused and one week later my parents were dead. Sheriff Banfield said it was an accident and the case was closed. Of course, how does one explain why his wagon was pulled 100 yards thru the woods by his horse, only to crash on a huge boulder."

"At the time, I decided to maintain my existence and continue raising chickens for meat and eggs. I had not anticipated the losing of 150 chickens within two days. By the time I realized the feed had been poisoned, it was too late. Since then, I went thru my parents' savings, and within two years, I am now here. Klaus knew I would eventually be ready to sell with the majority of my chickens dead. I now expect him any day to make me a ridiculous low offer, but I'll have to take it."

"When I took an inventory today, I opened a closet and found it full of books. How come?"

"My father was a Literature professor, and he emigrated here with a partial library. I have some great classics and best books of the 19th century. Look at my library list, just to mention a few"

Charles Dickens—Tale of two cities and Great Expectations
Herman Melville—Moby Dick
Henry David Thoreau—Walden, On civil disobedience
Charles Darwin—On the origin of species
Nathaniel Hawthorne—Scarlet letter, House of Seven Gables
Jane Austin—Pride and Prejudice
Emily Bronte—Wuthering Heights
Victor Hugo—Les Miserables
Marc Twain—Adventures of Huckleberry Finn
Charles Dickens—A Christmas Carrol

Dime novelists such as Ned Buntline, Edward Ellis and Prentiss Ingraham.

"The classics are not simple books like dime novels. How much education do you have?"

"I went to the town school till the 10th grade."

"So, with these books, you've self-educated yourself into a secondary level, heh? I suppose you've read them all!"

"Oh yes, and some twice. Now, it's your turn, tell me about you and why you're here."

"I was raised in Waco Texas. My dad was sheriff and after my 10th year in school, I became one of his deputies for about one year. I resigned when I found out that I could not hunt outlaws beyond the Waco's jurisdiction. For the next months I was a solo bounty hunter and amassed a small fortune in bounty rewards. After four months in the Denver Lawman School, I joined the US Marshal Service as a newbie on a confrontational squad. Over several months I advanced to Sargent and became the squad's leader. That brings us to why I'm here."

"You see Hannah, Rose Sanders was my sister."

Hannah was taken back and finally softly spoke, "Oh Jake, I'm so sorry for your loss, George and Rose were my friends and I so miss them."

"So do I. Officially, I'm here to find their murderer and put a stop to the robberies and murders of homesteaders along the ten miles east of New Braunfels."

"Well, I can help you with that. Klaus' ranch is ten miles from town, and he owns all the land except mine and the Sanders' ranch. His highway men caused so many depredations that the homesteaders all sold out and left the area."

"I suspected as much, but I have to prove it. Do you have any idea why Klaus wanted all this land and still wants ours?"

"Certainly do. If you ride over my 640 acres, you'll find several locations where a black greasy ooze seeps out of the ground—OIL"

"Oh really, but why does he need our four sections of land, he has more than he needs?"

"It's not for cattle. My father explained this

before he was killed. This entire area east of town is sitting on a huge prehistoric reservoir of organic matter. Today, after millions of years under pressure, it is crude oil. The reservoir underneath our land is the same reservoir under Klaus's land. So, if he has a well producing 100 barrels a day and you dig a well which produces 50 barrels a day, then his well's production may drop to as much as 50 barrels a day—in theory."

"I see, he wants it all."

"So, he thinks, but he's an idiot, the oil reservoir probably covers hundreds of miles if not most of Texas."

"With your knowledge, tell me about the town of New Braunfels."

"Sure, situated 30 miles east of San Antonio and 50 miles west of Austin, the town is a major trading and support center for our homesteaders and ranchers. The railroad has allowed the town to flourish and cattle can be loaded to cars without the extra distance to other railheads."

"It all started in 1845 when German immigrants landed by ship in Galveston. Making their way northwest, they realized that they could not make it in time, before winter, to their promised land far north of this present spot. So, they decided to stop, build cabins, cultivate fields and plant crops before the winter. The rest is history."

"I noticed today that several merchants bear German names."

"Yes, that is understandable. I may add that this community not only flourished because of the railroad. It grew because the German folks wanted to integrate with the locals. Over the years most Germans have lost the 'JA' or the 'V.' Now using Yes and the 'W.' Except for the people 's German names, you can't tell a person's heritage."

"Tomorrow, we're going to town to file a complaint and do some shopping. How is the town laid out?"

"The town is very clean despite its population of 2,000. The four principal streets are divided in north-south-east-west. The center of town is where the courthouse is located. As we arrive in the eastern sector, this is where we will do all our business. The western sector is mostly saloons, bawdy houses, dance halls, laundries and opium dens. The northern sector is for industries and the railroad yard. The southern sector is for rental housing and private homes."

"Well, it has been a pleasant evening, but it's time to get some sleep. I'll bring my horse to the barn and bed down in the hay."

"I don't think so. It will get cold tonight and we'll need the fire going in the stove. You can bring your bed roll and blanket and sleep on the floor. I will still have my privacy in the sectioned off area called my bedroom."

"Aren't you afraid what the town biddies will say about some improprieties?"

"I've never worried too much about what people think. What is the issue? That you're going to have your way with me! Heck, you could have done that earlier today and gotten away with it. Besides, I'll feel much safer knowing you're in the cabin. Leave me your bedroll and blanket and I'll prepare your bed with a pillow and the mattress I used for years."

Jake walked his horse to the barn. Took off the saddle and brushed him down. The oats bin was empty and there was very little hay left but a large supply of straw. He fed all the hay to both horses, filled the water trough and left—but not failing to notice how Hannah's horse was showing his ribs. On his way back, he stopped at the chicken coop and noticed how skinny and low energy the fifty chickens were. The barrel of chicken mash was empty but there was plenty of straw on the floor.

Arriving at the cabin, Jake noticed that Hannah was already in her nightgown and bathrobe. She had the stove banked with firewood and Jake's bed was all made. Before moving to her bed, she asked, "what is the agenda for tomorrow?"

"We're going to take your buckboard and horse and go shopping after we file a complaint at the sheriff's office. I can see several more things that you need in the cabin, chicken coop and barn."

***

During the night, the fire had gone down and the cabin got chilly. Jake got up and rebuilt the fire. Getting back in bed, he was stunned to find Hannah snugging up and hogging most of the blanket. Initially, she was shivering but quickly fell asleep as Jake and the room warmed up.

At first light, a rooster went cock-a-doodle-do. Hannah woke up and said, "I should have put that nuisance in the pot a long time ago." Without missing a step, she sat up as Jake said, "what would those bible thumpers say if they only knew where you spent half the night, next to a man in his union suit?"

"I don't much care, at least I was nice and warm with a wool blanket and two heating stoves at my service. How about some breakfast as your pay, heh?"

"Great, let's get dressed. I'll cook the bacon, you put the beans to reheat and make some coffee. I'm sure we can find some eggs to finish the menu, heh."

Jake was quickly at the stove cooking. Hannah took longer to get dressed. When she came out of the bedroom, she was wearing a riding skirt and blouse. She was carrying her new boots as she said, "I think Mr. Wolfgang made a mistake and gave me either two right or two left boots."

"No, those are brogans. Both boots are neutral. You wear them and they will form fit to your feet. Eventually you'll have a right and a left, heh."

"Oh, Ok. By the way, doing my ablutions was such a pleasure with the accessories you got me."

With a piece of bacon on his fork he said, "what in heck are ablutions?"

"You know, washing my face, brushing my teeth, brushing my hair, the things you do every morning?"

"Oh, really. I just go to the privy! Something tells me that hanging around you will give me a new vocabulary!"

Hannah smiled and thought—*that man is going to get more than new words. He's going to find out what it's like to end up caring for someone more than your own self and how good a catch I turn out to be.*

During breakfast, Jake asked how the

chickens were doing and how the egg production was holding up. Hannah answered, "I haven't been able to support myself since the poisoning. The leftover chickens were stressed from a partial poisoning and so egg production has almost stopped. Without eggs to sell, I cannot buy chicken mash to feed them and so the vicious cyle begins again—damned if you do and damned if you don't."

"Well, we're going to do something about that today. If you clean up the dishes, I'll go harness your large gelding and we'll be off."

With the buckboard ready, Jake went in the house to get Hannah. She had added some red lip cream, facial rouge, her Bulldog, and her new cowboy hat. Jake couldn't help but let out a soft whistle and say, "Ma'am you look great."

Stepping off the porch, Jake decided he wanted to see what Hannah could do shooting a Bulldog. He set up a man size target at 5 yards and had her shoot off 5 rounds in quick self-defense mode. Jake was more than impressed in Hannah's determination and expertise. He then set an old pail at 15 yards and Hannah managed to hit it with all five shots. Jake simply smiled and said, "Wow, you have nothing to fear of salacious men, you can take care of yourself."

On the short trip to town, they covered the mile in no time. Arriving at the sheriff's office, they entered without knocking. The sheriff stood up and said, "oh, it's you again." Jake looked around and, finding the jail cells empty, asked where his three prisoners were. Sheriff Banfield said, "our prosecutor, Desmond Beltzer, said he would not prosecute them on hearsay. So, the town bought them some new clothes and I had to let them go."

Jake was trying to control himself and so asked if he could see the investigation report on his sister's death. Sheriff Banfield responded, "they were shot dead without witnesses, and that's the end of it."

Jake let it all out. "You dingbat, you knew that I and the victim would be filing a complaint this morning. Yet, you failed to do your job like you failed to investigate my sister's murder." Jake stepped forward and grabbed the sheriff by his shirt's collar, lifted him off the floor and slapped him across the face to get his attention.

"Omer Banfield, as a US Marshall, I charge you with malfeasance and obstruction of justice. You will be prosecuted and will go to prison."

Jake then ripped the sheriff's badge off and pushed the sheriff violently in a jail cell where he landed on the floor. The sheriff was screaming that he had no authority to arrest him and would be released by the prosecutor.

Jake ignored the ranting sheriff and turned to look at the deputy. "Deputy Bixby, I'm aware of the letter, you and the judge, sent to Captain Ennis. I suspect you're honest. Are you willing and capable of taking on the extra responsibility of sheriff?"

"Yes sir. Without a doubt, this office will become respectable again."

Jake swore Herb Bixby as sheriff. Afterwards, he said, "do you know where these three 'would be rapists' went?"

"Yes, they're at Billy Joe's Bar having breakfast and several whiskeys. I'm sure they're waiting for their boss, Kurt Klaus, since they didn't get back to the ranch last night. Apparently, Weber's Livery would not let them have their horses back when they could not pay the $3 fee."

"Keep their cells ready, they'll be back."

Jake walked back to the saloon at a brisk walk. Almost forgetting that Hannah was following him, he stopped at the batwing doors and said, "stay with me like a tail on a horse and keep your hand on your bulldog."

Jake walked in and straight to the regulators' table. He pulled out a 11-inch leather item and hit each in the head without warning. All three men fell in their plates like they had each received a bullet to the back of the head. Jake spoke up, "I'm a US Marshal and placing these three animals under arrest. I'll give any man $3 to drag them back to the jail where you are to strip them down to their union suits and take off their boots. You are also welcomed to keep their clothes and boots." Within minutes the bar emptied out. Jake then asked the bartender the damage to cover the food and whiskey. "No damage, Kurt Klaus will cover their tab."

Walking this time to the Courthouse.

Hannah asked, "what was that black leather strap you hit them with. They dropped as if a tree fell on their heads."

"That was a 'sap', not a strap. It's a double layered leather strip with a metal flexible band inside, and with a ball of lead at the tip. You swing it at the wrist and the accelerated velocity hits hard as a train. You can accomplish the same with a pistol, but it doesn't leave bleeding cuts and it is a rather quiet method of rendering someone unconscious."

"Hum, sounds like a nice Christmas present to make to a lady, huh?" Jake smiled and thought of an answer but would wait till another time—when their encounter was more than 24 hours old.

Walking in the courthouse, Jake headed to the probate office. He showed the clerk a copy of George and Rose Sanders will, showed his credentials, and requested a court order to change the registered deed into his name.

He then headed for the Judge's office. He explained to the court clerk that he needed a court order to sell off the outlaws' horses and firearms.

His last stop was the prosecutor's office. Walking in without knocking, he stepped up to Desmond Beltzer and said, "the only way to get a mule's attention is to hit them on the head with a 2X4." Beltzer looked confused and said, "who are you and what do you want." Without hesitation, Jake grabbed Beltzer's starched collar, stood him up, and landed an impressive round-house punch to his nose. Beltzer fell back in his chair with the look of horror on his face.

Jake said, "I'm the US Marshal who arrested the three Klaus cowhands for attempted rape and this is Miss Bauer, the intended victim."

Beltzer yelled out, "I'm not prosecuting Klaus's men on the word of an outsider and a bimbo."

Hannah knew that the best of Jake was about to explode again. Jake put his hand behind Beltzer's head and slammed his face onto the top of his desk. "You numskull, this lady is one of your townsfolks, this is Hannah Bauer, the intended victim. Get up, you're going to jail. As a US Marshal, I charge you with malfeasance and obstruction of justice."

Prodding Beltzer out of his office, Judge Aiken came up to them and said, "Officer Harrison, your court orders will be available after lunch and will be delivered to Mr. Werner and the town clerk. Also, get me and attorney with sand and I'll hold trials on the attempted rapists, Banfield, Beltzer and even the Klaus clan."

"I will find one and thank you for your letter with Herb to Captain Ennis. First, I need to get the proof to prosecute Klaus."

Once at the sheriff's office, he shoved Beltzer in the same cell with Banfield and the three Klaus cowhands were in the other cell. Jake says to Sheriff Bixby, "don't let these men out of their cell under any circumstance. They use the pot for their functions, and you use the floor panel to pass the pot and their food. To protect you against Hans Klaus threatening you, give me all the keys. If he or any of his men break the cell lock, they will be arrested as well. I mean business and will get a new prosecutor to bring this bunch of cowards to justice."

"Don't worry, they'll all be here when you

return. And thanks for your help. It's about time we overturn the criminal element in this town."

Jake and his 'tail' stepped three buildings down to send a telegram.

Jake wrote his note and handed it to the telegrapher:

> **To Captain Ennis**
> **US Marshal Service—Denver, Co**
> **From US Marshal Harrison, New Braunfels, Tx**
> **REQUESTING A GUN TOTING ATTORNEY STOP NEED TO PROSECUTE SHERIFF AND PROSECUTOR FOR MALFEASANCE STOP MURDERER KNOWN BUT STILL AT LARGE STOP**

Jake told the telegrapher that he would wait for an answer. Whispering to Hannah, he said, "this assures me that the message was properly sent to the right place. Fifteen minutes later the machine started clacking away. The message read:

From Capt. Ennis to US Marshal Harrison
Attorney Clifton Gibson will arrive in two days STOP
Assigned to the resolution of murders STOP

Jake looked at the telegrapher and said, "you are the only man in town who knows of this. If Hans Klaus knows of this before the attorney's arrival, I will come and see you and you'll be on your way to Huntsville State Prison for a vacation. Is that clear?"

"Very clear, Marshal."

Back on the boardwalk, Jake says, "sorry you had to see all this, but I had promised you to never leave you unprotected, so it had to be."

"Well, being the tail on a horse has been somewhat entertaining. It was nice to see some justice being dispatched."

"How about some lunch. There's a diner across the street."

"Jake, I'm a bit embarrassed to say, but I've never been in a diner."

"Yeah, that's another example of the 'tin plate and the spoon.'"

Entering Bessie's Diner, the couple was seated at a private table. After checking out the menu, Hannah asked what veal cutlets, fried steaks and buffalo tongues were. With an explanation, Hannah ordered their house specialty onion soup, and veal cutlets, mashed potatoes, sliced carrots, buttered rolls, tea and ice cream for dessert. Jake had the same but with coffee and added an extra cutlet for them to share.

Waiting for their meal, Jake asked Hannah if she enjoyed caring for chickens and selling eggs for a living. Hannah answered, "Yes, I miss the day when I had 200 chickens and was selling eggs to three different mercantile in town."

"Can your chicken coop handle so many laying hens."

"Oh yes, it has plenty of perches and laying

boxes. I am convinced that there is no money in raising chicks and keeping roosters around. A brooding hen usually spends a week or more collecting a clutch and then broods for three weeks. After the chicks hatch, she lays fertilized eggs for another two weeks, which is not a good idea when selling eggs. All in all, she is out of production for almost eight weeks. Then we have to keep the chicks in 85-95 degrees Fahrenheit for weeks. Plus, we have to feed roosters year-round and listen to their cock-a-doodle every morning. If I had my way, I'd only keep laying hens and replace one third of my flock every year."

"I like your plan, and I can make this happen if you'll let me?"

Jake let his hand cover Hannah's who said, "only if we share the enterprise together."

"I'd be happy to."

The two ended up looking at each other in total silence while holding hands. Reality came back when their thoughts were interrupted as the onion soup arrived.

Hannah had never had onion soup and could

not believe how tasty it was. She mentioned, "I wish I had the recipe, since I have bushels of large onions left in the garden. I cannot feed them to the chickens because it flavors the eggs and customers don't like that."

When the main meal arrived, they ate in silence. Hannah was smiling and expressing her satisfaction by intermittent moans. Without asking, Jake placed the extra veal cutlet in Hannah's plate. The ice cream put an icing on the meal. Finishing with more tea and coffee, Jake asked, "how do you feed vegetables to your chickens?"

"My pa recognized years ago, that with 200 hens, a 2-acre garden provided a nutritional supplement to chicken mash. He bought a manual grinder and I put everything, leaves, plants and roots in the grinder. It all comes out as fine chips which the chickens can swallow and love."

"Are there any vegetables that you cannot feed them?"

"Yes, the ones that make chickens ill are: green potato peals, tomatoes, raw beans, moldy plants, apple seeds and coffee grounds."

"Wow, there is more to caring for simple birds than I ever realized. I have a lot to learn."

"I also have a lot to learn, and I hope we can learn together."

"I'd like that. For now, let's run our errands."

There first place was the Wolfgang Mercantile. Walking on the boardwalk holding hands, Jake noticed three men walking with a swagger, and heading for them. Hannah whispers, "that is Kurt Klaus and his two sycophants." As they got up close, they started whistling and hollering. Klaus then yells, "hey that's a nice honey on your arms, I bet she has a nice honeypot!"

Jake took offense and said, "it's obvious you don't recognize this lady, this is Hannah Bauer, my girlfriend. It's not proper to throw catcalls at a lady, so apologize or I'll see to it that you never whistle again."

"Who's going to make me. There is three of us and we're not backing down."

As Klaus placed his hand on his gun, Jake never hesitated. With a gloved hand he popped Klaus in the mouth and both his front teeth came falling out. "Now apologize or the next punch will flatten your nose and the pain to get it straighten out will make you pee yourself."

"Sorry Ma'am, I didn't recognize you."

Jake then opens his vest to show his US Marshal's badge. "Now go tell your daddy that, as Rose Sanders brother, I'm now the owner of the Double S ranch. I've been assigned here to investigate their murder, and I'll be seeing your pa and you again. Just so you're clear, you have three of your regulators in jail for attempting to rape Miss Bauer, and that's where they'll stay pending their trial. If you try to collect their horses and firearms from Werner's Livery, I'll come and arrest you since they are now under the control of the court. I hope your day gets better, heh."

The three men simply turned around and walked away. Hannah looked at Jake and said, "so I'm now your girlfriend, huh?" "Let's just say that we're working on that, Ma'am," as he took her hand and walked into the mercantile.

Helga greeted them and clearly saw the hand holding. "We need some more things.

Hannah will pick out some extra vittles and spices, and I'd like some new assorted cooking pots, a large and small cast iron frying pan, a kitchen clock, a complete set of kitchen butcher and paring knives, a set of porcelain dishes and cups, a set of water glasses, basins for doing dishes, soap for cleaning dishes, and a set of steel pails."

During the gathering, Jake asked Herman, "Hannah will be expanding her chicken flock. How many dozen eggs can you handle?"

"I could easily handle six dozen every other day. I also have two competitors who could handle the same amount—like when her pa was alive. I would be willing to pay 30 cents a dozen. There is a big demand for fresh eggs which will increase if the supply is regular. The only thing is the handling and delivery. We have a wood working shop that could make you a flat that holds six dozen at a time. Each egg would have its own slot and you could cushion them with wood shavings. Ideally, it would be nice if the flat was left on the counter and replaced every other day with the next flat. This would ease the display and the breakage from customers looking for the bigger eggs."

Hannah came back with all the ingredients to make a cake and many other dry goods. She also included a flour sifter, saltshaker, rolling pin and a cutting board. The entire order came up to $31.78 which was entered in Hannah's credit booklet. After loading everything in the buckboard, they headed to Heinz's Hardware and Feed Store.

While tying the horse to the railing, Jake asked, "how come the streets are clean of horse manure. Every town I've been in has the messiest streets full of fresh, compacted, and dry manure infested with flies. How is it possible to have such clean streets?"

"That is old German heritage and pride. Look down the street, see that wagon being loaded. That is a manure spreader and the street sweeper is filling it as he does every morning and late afternoon. When it's full, they spread it on homesteaders' gardens and fields for a cheap price."

"Really, where can I order one of those spreaders?"

"Right here at the hardware store."

Hannah introduced Jake to Herbert Heinz. Herbert in turn said, "and whom may you be Ma'am?" "Why Mr. Heinz, I'm Hannah Bauer, you've known me all my life." Realizing he had bolloxed that situation, he thought better to keep digging the hole any deeper and changed the subject. "How may I help you?"

Jake took over. "We'd like to purchase laying hens since we're expanding the Bauer's egg business."

"Do you want pullets, young layers or mature layers?"

Hannah answered, "young layers but not younger than nine months since anything younger lays pullet eggs which are small and sometimes without a yolk."

"Good choice. I agree 'fart' eggs without a yolk are not appreciated by customers. What variety and how many would you like?"

Hannah continued. "Forty Rhode Island Reds, forty White Leghorn, forty Plymouth

Rock (black with white stripes) and forty brown Buffington."

"It's clear you know what you're doing, Hannah. Those are the best layers, and the variety gives you a better resistance to disease. I can have them here in two days by train from San Antonio. Just set up an account with Finneus Barclay's freighting company. He'll cover his freight wagon with chicken wire and deliver them right in your coop."

Hannah added, "today I need ten feed and water trays, 100 pounds of chicken mash, 100 pounds of layer pellets and 50 pounds of fine oyster shells. Jake added, plus we need five bales of your best hay for horses, 100 pounds of oats, and two bales of wood shavings. We'll take all this with us in the buckboard. Then prepare a big order and arrange for Mr. Barclay to deliver it to the Bauer's barn to include: 500 pounds of chicken mash, 500 pounds of layer pellets, 200 pounds of fine oyster shells, 25 bales of good horse hay, 200 pounds of oats, 20 bales of wood shavings and 10 bales of straw. Everything goes in the barn and the hay goes in the loft."

The last item is a manure spreader. Order it and deliver it to my ranch, the old George and Rose Sanders ranch."

"What size—small, medium or large. The small is for a small farmer, the large is for long distance hauling. The medium is for crop farmers."

"In that case, the medium one."

"Anything else?"

"No sir."

"Well, that an extremely large order. How may I ask are you planning to uh......uh

"Pay for it? Not a problem. I would like to set up two accounts. One for Miss Bauer and one for my ranch. Here are two $500 bank drafts, off your own Ranchers Bank, which will likely get things started."

After loading the buckboard, they went to see Mr. Barclay to set up an account for both locations. Each account was opened with a $100 deposit.

Their last stop was the town clerk's office. With the court order, the paperwork was quickly done, and Jake left with his copy of the new deed. He also paid the taxes of $229 for the current year.

As they were stepping to the buckboard, Jake saw someone entering Billy Joe's Saloon—a man who would change both their lives forever.

***

CHAPTER 8

LIFE IN NEW BRAUNFELS

"Hannah, I just saw an old friend and classmate from the Lawman School enter Billy Joe's Saloon. Let's go say hello."

After a short walk, next to the batwing doors, Jake looks at Hannah and was about to say... "I know, pretend I'm the tail again." Once inside, his friend spotted him and walked over to give him a hug. Jake says, Willie, this is my uh, uh my woman, Hannah Bauer. Hannah, this is an old friend Willie Irving." Hannah stepped up and eagerly shook Willie's hand. Willie looked a bit surprised, but Jake intervened. "It's ok

Hannah, Willie is still surprised to find a white folk shaking his hand."

Willie asked them to have a seat while he stepped to the bar to get two beers and a glass of wine. While waiting for Willie, Hannah said, "so I've moved up from girlfriend to your woman, huh?"

"Go with it for now, you'll soon understand, heh."

Settling down to visit, Jake asked what Willey had been up to for the past year. "I've been bounty hunting solo. It's been very dangerous and have been shot twice because I give outlaws too many chances. Yet I've amassed a small fortune by local standards. I'm here to collect a bounty which is being processed by Sheriff Bixby. What about you, what are you doing here, so far from Denver?"

Jake covered the past year and the reason for his presence in Texas. He also covered info on Hannah and the tyrant rancher, Hans and Kurt Klaus. He included info on his family's murder and the murder of waylaid homesteaders.

Jake then added, "so what are your plans for next year?"

"You're not going to believe this, but it's time to quit this solo work. Without a backup, dangerous work will eventually be fatal. I'm thinking of applying to the US Marshal Service."

"Well let me make you an offer. Come work for me. I'll deputize you and you'll receive $100 a month from the Marshal Service. Every wanted outlaw you bring in with a reward is yours. I guarantee you that Klaus' regulators all have wanted posters on them. Your major responsibility is to first protect Hannah and secondly my ranch cowhands. You'll be staying in my ranch house, eat at the bunkhouse kitchen, but batching it otherwise. When I go after Klaus, we'll do it together. You will always have me, my foreman my cowhands or Hannah as your backup."

"Are you for real, you're my only friend. I'd do it anytime and without pay. You have a deal."

"Great, here is your badge, just lift your right hand and say, I do."

"I do!"

"Get yourself some snacks, coffee and whatever personal items you need and head out for the ranch. Here is a note of introduction for the Wolfgang Mercantile and my foreman, Clayton Briggs. Get acquainted with the boys and plan on coming to Hannah's place for breakfast tomorrow to plan our day. Welcome aboard."

After Willie left, Hannah said, "at first I thought you were color blind and was just polite with a black man. Then I realized you were really friends and not only that, but you offered him a job to protect me. That is really a feather in your hat, Marshal Harrison."

"Does that mean possible privileges?"

"GO WITH IT FOR NOW, you'll soon understand, heh!"

"Will do, just remember, Willie is a man you can trust 100%."

***

Their next stop was the other two mercantile Herman had mentioned. The first was the

Horst Lehman Mercantile. He recognized Hannah and was very willing to do the same arrangement as Herman. The other merchant was the Dieter Fischer Mercantile. Mr. Fischer greeted Hannah by saying, "please tell me you'll be bringing some eggs. My customers are very impatient, I can't find a source of fresh eggs."

"Yes, we'll be bringing you six dozen every other day, within a few weeks."

After arrangements were made, Hannah asked if he had any books. Mr. Fischer escorted her to a display. Hannah gasped as she picked up a few classics. Jake stepped in and said, "there are six choices, take all of them before they disappear."

As they were about to leave, Hannah spotted a special of the day. Again Mr. Fischer said, the owner of Bessie's Diner is selling her onion soup recipe for 25 cents. "I'll take one and I need all the ingredients to make it."

Finally, with a full buckboard, they headed back to the cabin. They held hands and never spoke. Arriving, Jake stepped down and came around to help Hannah down. Standing too close to the buckboard, Hannah slid and brushed Jake's body. Now being face to face, it finally happened. They gently touched lips and separated momentarily as both rushed into a passionate union with body to body and mouth to mouth. It was Jake who spoke first, "there was a lot of information in that kiss!" "Yes, it was meant to be, and I guess we both 'understand' each other, heh?"

After many trips to unload the household goods, they brought the buckboard to the barn and unloaded it. Together they fed the horses some oats, hay and water. Then they watered the chickens, fed them some chicken mash and set out a tray of fine oyster shells. In anticipation of the other chickens arriving, they cleaned the floor of straw/poop and added a generous layer of wood chips. Jake gathered a half dozen eggs for themselves, and Hannah headed to the garden to pick up six large onions. Then back to the cabin to make onion soup.

Meanwhile at the Circle K ranch, Kurt was explaining his contact with the US Marshal, the new owner of the Sanders' ranch, and the man involved with the Bauer girl. He also mentioned that he was looking for the Sanders' murderer and would be coming to the ranch to ask questions. To make it worse, he said that Sheriff Banfield and prosecutor Beltzer had been arrested for obstructing justice. Hans was surprised with the developments and Kurt saw that he was getting angry.

He finally broke his silence and first made it clear he was furious that Kurt now looked like a bum without his front teeth. Addressing his two sycophants, he said, "what good were you, you were supposed to protect my son. The next time you go to town Kurt, make sure you're escorted by two regulators, not some half-baked cowhands.

Now get out and fetch me the lead regulator, Bull Benninger."

Meeting with four regulators, Hans said, "we have a problem. There's a US Marshal asking questions. I want him dead and anyone with him, that includes the Bauer woman. I don't want any witnesses. Make it look like a robbery as usual. There's an extra hundred in it for each of you, if the job is done right. Now get on the road and wait for them before they go back to town tomorrow and cause more trouble."

Back at the Bauer cabin, Hannah was busy cutting up onions and adding all the ingredients. Setting the pot on the stove to slow cook, Hannah made a suggestion. "With the hens arriving tomorrow, I suggest we go to the coop where the hens are still busy eating the mash. We have to band their leg since they will be the first group to be butchered in a replacement rotation."

The process of banding all fifty chickens took about an hour. Afterwards, they started preparing supper of steaks, baked potatoes and cabbage salad. Hannah made a small cake for dessert. Jake was watching and never realized all the ingredients needed to make a cake— butter, sugar, eggs, flour, salt, milk and baking powder.

While drinking coffee, Jake said, "tell me more about the business of chickens and eggs."

"Ok, let's start with demand. Most people eat 250 eggs a year. It has become the most regular and popular breakfast item as fried, scrambled, omelets, sandwiches and as egg salad. It is also used for cooking, especially pastries, as you saw today. It is a commonly used hair shampoo. The big thing is that city folks don't have coops and so they need to buy them at the mercantiles."

"Maintaining production is a perpetual problem. Chickens stop laying in face of stress, daylight hours less than 12 hours a day, poor nourishment or cold temperatures. Good management with a secure coop takes care of stress and nourishment. The weather in south Texas helps with long daylight hours and warmer temperatures."

"Chickens have habits and health issues. They need to scratch and peck. That's why I have a run where I throw corn and other seeds for them to scratch the ground to find them. You recall that I grow squash. They have wet meat and don't grind well. But they hang well, and chickens love to peck at them for the meat. As far as health issues, they get diarrhea easily and can die from it. They are susceptible to Mareks disease which is an untreatable infection. The strangest thing is that a perfectly healthy chicken can drop dead with what the experts call a heart attack. But all in all, they are a friendly and tough bird."

"That's all great information. I have many questions and several categories I'll want to cover with you. But, for now, we have time for one more subject before supper. Tell me what is specific about a coop."

"A coop must be large enough to

accommodate the number of chickens you have. A chicken needs a minimum of 2 sq. ft. of space or 100 chickens need 200 sq. ft. which means a 10X20 coop. Mine holds 200 chickens which is why it's 10X40 feet. The run requires 8 sq, ft. per bird which is why my pa built the run 400X400 ft., or 1600 sq. ft."

"Now let's walk thru the coop. Upon entering you see the perches. The perches are 2-inch round poles set 24 inches off the floor and 18 inches apart. A chicken needs 10 inches of space along the perch. Next are the laying boxes. Mine are 10 inches deep and 16 inches wide. The box is bedded with straw and each box has a slanted roof to prevent chickens from standing on the box where they will poop and make a mess. You need a minimum of one box per 2 layers as long as you collect the eggs twice a day. The feed and water trays need to be 8 inches off the floor. That prevents rodents from eating the feed and prevents chickens from scratching the mash out of the trays or pooping in the trays. The last thing is the coop's bedding. The wood chips you ordered is probably the best. It keeps the chicken's feet dry, keeps the poop dry and is easy to clean up and exchange. Straw is second choice but messy and a lot of work as you saw."

"Sounds like a well laid out coop. Is there anything you would add to make it handier?"

"Yes, an attached insulated work area to store the eggs from heat, and a worktable to prepare them for shipping."

"Great, well I'm starved, what do you say we have supper?"

Supper started with the onion soup. Hannah was so pleased with the recipe that she promised to keep planting onions for cooking and soup. The main menu was fried steaks, baked potatoes, coleslaw and a fine cake for dessert. Jake made the mistake of raving how nice it was to have a home cooked meal and Hannah jumped on the occasion by saying, "Home cooked meals come with a woman around the house, hey?"

"I know, I'm working on that, Ma'am!"

After cleaning the kitchen, they settled down on the couch to read. Hannah had one of her new books and Jake was working on one of Hannah's books about raising chickens. An hour went by as Jake put his book down and took Hannah's away. "That's it, I can't concentrate anymore. I just want to hold you. Hannah must have been thinking the same, as both jumped in each other's arms. The kissing changed to passionate necking till Hannah said, "this is all new to me and I can't seem to get enough of you."

"Well, if it seems right, then it is right. But for now, we had better stop before things get out of hand. Let's go to bed, we have a busy day scheduled tomorrow."

Hannah went into the bedroom to change in her nightshirt as Jake set his bed up on the floor next to the kitchen stove. Hannah came back to give Jake a goodnight kiss as Jake said, "lady, you know you're going to join me when you get cold, so why don't you just join me now and get settled in?" "So now, I'm a lady, heh? Well a lady doesn't do those things!"

"These things are allowed when a couple is falling in love."

Hannah never hesitated, she laid down and kissed Jake without a further spoken word.

Despite the temptation, both fell asleep in each other's arms.

With a morning cock-a-doodle-do, both awoke. Hannah got up and rushed to the privy as Jake went to the chicken coop to relieve himself and come back with another handful of eggs to feed the extra mouth—Willie was coming to breakfast. Hannah was already cooking the bacon and had started a batch of oatmeal as well as bread to toast. Jake took out another frying pan, added bacon fat and started cracking eggs on the frying pan's edge. Suddenly he said, "what the hell, this egg wont crack open."

"You silly man, you picked up a wooden eggs.

"A what?"

"I randomly leave wooden eggs in the laying boxes to discourage the hens from eating eggs. Pecking on a wooden eggs trains them to leave eggs alone!"

"Oh, must be I haven't gotten to that chapter yet."

As breakfast was ready, Willie showed up. He clearly had something to say but when he saw the spread, he just sat down and started to eat. At the end of breakfast, Willie started.

"Riding over here, I saw four riders coming from a mile away. Not wanting a confrontation, I hid behind trees. As they passed by, it was clear they were well healed. Letting them pass, I went on my way. Shortly later, I looked back and saw them returning on the trail. It is obvious they are looking for you and it's not for a social visit."

"We'll be ready. Hannah and I will be riding the buckboard and you will ride on our left. If a gunfight is inevitable, I'll take the two on the right and you take the two on the left. Hannah will be our backup with her shotgun. In case they send a rider to flank us, she will move to the back of the buckboard and protect our backs."

After breakfast, Hannah cleaned up the kitchen, Willie harnessed the gelding to the buckboard, and Jake fed and watered the chickens. Getting on their way, it didn't take long for three riders to be headed their way. Hannah move to the back and was ready.

Stopping to meet the suspected highwaymen, the leader pulled his pistol and said, "this is a robbery. Give me your money or you'll die."

Jake answered, "what is going to happen, as he showed his US Marshal badge, is that you're all under arrest. Put your hands up or get ready to meet your maker. What happened was as expected. The other two outlaws went for their pistols as the leader cocked his pistol. Another situation of kill or be killed. Jake and Willie drew and fired as all three highwaymen were knocked off their horses. As the smoke cleared, Hannah let go both barrels at a boulder, as a man's face was peppered with 00 Buckshot. Hannah was thrown off balance by the double blast and found herself laying down on the buckboard's floor.

Willie commented, "Jeez….that's not a woman to cross, my friend."

After securing all four highwaymen to their horses, they moved along to Sheriff Bixby's office.

Sheriff Bixby checked the four dead men and said, "I'll check their pockets for some identification, check the wanted posters and ask Sam Cooper, bartender at Billy Joe's, to check them out in case he might know their names. Check back with me later today."

"Willie, entertain yourself and we'll meet here at 3 o'clock."

The Duo then went to Werner's Livery. "Frank, you can now sell the three horses from the accused rapists and the four we have at the sheriff's office, also with the Circle K brand."

"I've been checking with Judge Aiken. We've decided to send all the Circle K brand horses to my brother in San Antonio where the brand isn't known. I also have a gun-shop owner, Barney Blackwell, who is desperate to buy all these guns since his deliveries are backed up."

Jake could see Hannah admiring a light tan mare. "In that case, make the deals and pay yourself with a 10% commission. Is that mare for sale?"

"Sure is, she's a beauty that is gentle, a good rider and smart."

"How much?"

"Eighty dollars with a new saddle, and 5% commission would be adequate."

Jake pays Frank and says, "Hannah, let's saddle her because she's now your horse and you'll have to name her."

"Oh Jake, I've never had my own horse, are you sure, that's a lot of money."

"Yes, now we can go riding and leave the buckboard at home."

***

Their next stop was the Cass Construction office. Hannah asked why they were stopping there. "It's a surprise but be my tail and add your ideas whenever I miss something."

"Hello, my name is Cecil Cass, how may I help you?" After introductions, Jake started, the Bauer homestead needs assistance. Bring several squares of cedar shingles and repair the roof of the cabin, chicken coop and barn. Then add an addition to the chicken coop next to the entry door. Make it 10X15 with plenty of two-foot deep shelves, a large 36- inch-high worktable and leave room for six bales of shavings/straw.

Plus add a hand pump well in the addition and insulate all the walls to keep eggs fresh." As Hannah was stepping away to look at a steel contraption, Jake whispered to Cecil, "and measure the coop and all its perches and laying boxes since you'll be building one just like it later on, and keep this quiet, heh. For the last change, extend the chicken run to one acre in size with four-foot walls of chicken wire and separate it into three paddocks.

Hannah was standing there in total disbelief. She finally spoke and said, "it looks like you want to become a chicken farmer, Mr. Marshal?"

Jake asked, "did I forget anything?"

"No, except what is this steel contraption for?"

Mr. Cass answered, "that's a slaughtering funnel. It's actually an inverted funnel where you invert a chicken, drop it in the funnel, and only its head/neck sticks out from the bottom. When you cut the head off, the bird stays put, and the blood is collected in a bucket. My men in the wood shop built it for a customer."

"Jake, can we have six of them?"

"Of course, now we need a flat that holds six

dozen of eggs. Each egg needs its own pocket which we'll partially fill with wood shavings. The flats need to be stackable and with plenty of space between the egg and the next flat. We'll need six flats to start with, and likely more in the future. Most important, keep the flats as light but durable as possible."

"Not a problem, I have three retired lifelong woodworkers who work on these projects and are paid by a percentage of the proceeds. They'll be happy with these two orders of funnels and flats."

"Now when you're done with the Bauer homestead, I want you to go to my ranch, the old Sanders ranch, and dig me a well and install a windmill pump. I want piped in water to the kitchen and water closet. Plus, install a coal fired hot water boiler to provide piped in hot water to the kitchen and water closet bathtub and wash sink. Keep the hand pump for the next project, heh?"

"Very good, my men will start on the roof work today and the chicken coop tomorrow."

Walking on the boardwalk, Hannah asked,

"why are you putting so much money in your ranch when you mentioned that you might sell it?"

"These improvements will keep their value on a sale. If I don't sell it, I'll be able to enjoy it."

Their next stop was the wagon shop. Jake asked what was new in buckboards. "We have the new spring-loaded seats and axles. The back has 14-inch-high walls and a dropdown tailgate. It is rugged but it gives a very smooth ride. It also comes with a retractable rain bonnet."

"Smooth enough to deliver eggs?"

"Yes sir."

"How much to trade for that old buckboard?

"Sixty dollars."

"Done, put our harness horse on it."

Hannah whispered, "Our horse? Does that mean. . . . . . . ?"

"Yes, our horse and buggy, go with it for now, dear. We'll discuss this later." "For sure, dear. . . . .!"

Their next stop was at the Bromley Freight Company. "Hello, my name is Adelbert, the owner. How may I help you and people call me Bert." After introductions, Jake opened an account and Bert told them that their chickens were arriving in an hour. His men were adding sawdust to the wagons and covering them with chicken wire. Jake added, "fine, we'll go for lunch and we'll be back home before you arrive."

Lunch at Bessie's Diner was a feast of meatloaf, mashed potatoes, fried onions with plenty of coffee. After a rice pudding dessert and coffee, they went to the sheriff's office where Willie was waiting. The four bodies had been identified and each had a bounty of $500. Jake gave Willie two of the vouchers to divide the rewards evenly. Willie objected and said, "but boss, I can only account for one of the outlaws."

"No, we rely on each other, and from now on we divide the rewards evenly. So, for now, let's throw the bodies in the buckboard and you and I will deliver them personally to Hans Klaus today. Hannah will stay at home since her new 160 chickens are arriving today."

***

Arriving home, the Cass carpenters were busy on the roofs. Jake said, if you're not comfortable staying here alone, you can come with us."

"No, I need to be here when the hens arrive. Besides the lead carpenter, Elliot Billings, was a good friend of my pa. I trust him and can always rely on him if visitors arrive. Just be safe and come back to me."

After Jake and Willie continued on, two altered freighting wagons arrived. The clucking sounds were a continuous buzz in the air. As directed, the wagon was backed up to the coop's door to unload the birds. During the process one of the freighters accidentally opened the latch on the rooster's door. The rooster rushed in the chicken coop. When Hannah saw what was happening, she stopped the transfer and said, I don't want any fertilized eggs, so catch that rooster and hand it to me. The ax is waiting, and he'll be in the pot for supper."

After the freighters left, Hannah filled the water trays till all the birds had their fill. She added some layer pellets and after the birds had gotten acquainted with the perches and laying boxes, she opened the door to the outside run. There she threw some oats and corn on the ground for them to scratch and forage. To accommodate so many birds, she added several elevated watering buckets scattered in the run. The last chore was to process the rooster. Processing only one bird, a modified technique was used. She skinned the breast area and popped the breast meat out. She also skinned the legs and thighs. The meat was then added to a boiling pot. Later she would make gravy, add vegetables and cook a chicken pie for supper.

Meanwhile, Jake and Willie were making good time to the Circle K ranch. Arriving on the access road, Jake stopped the buckboard and said, "we are here to deliver Klaus' regulators and confront him with his alleged robbery involvement. We are not looking for an arrest or for a fight. But we are not backing down. I'll do the talking and ask you to stand with a loaded and cocked shotgun at cowboy-arms. I'm hoping that the badge and shotgun will be enough for his toadies to stand-down."

Moving to the house's front door, Jake and Willie were somewhat surprised to see such a massive two-story stone house and outbuildings. Jake wondered how such opulence was possible on a cattle ranch. It suggested some illegal activities to support such an enterprise. Jake was taken out of his reverie when Kurt Klaus opened the front door and said with a lisp, "what are you two ass holes during on this ranch, get out!"

"We are here to drop off your regulators and talk to your father. Now we can do it peaceably or we can go inside and do it with force."

"Wait here." As they were waiting, three men showed up who were not cowpokes. Eventually, a pot-bellied smug face with an arrogant swagger stepped on the porch. "What do you two saddle bums want, I'm a busy man."

"If you're not a blind idiot, you'll notice by our badge that we are US Marshals, not saddle bums."

"So what? State your business, you're beginning to bore me."

"First, here are your regulators who tried to kill us."

"Never saw them before."

"Strange that they were riding horses with the Circle K brand. Kind of stupid if you ask me."

"They were stolen horses; I want them back."

"Not possible, they are already on their way to San Antonio where they will be sold as property of the US Marshal Service."

"Secondly, you've had your regulators run roughshod over the homesteaders. Fear has pushed them to sell out to you without thinking. Well, you're not getting the Bauer homestead and the Sanders' ranch, which I now own. We will both be getting our share of the oil reservoir under the land. So, you can take your threats and go pound sand."

"Thirdly, I know you're responsible for ordering the murder of my sister and brother-in-law. Although I can't yet prove it, I eventually will. When I do, I assure you that it will suck to be you. You'll be going to the hoosegow and the shooter will hang."

Klaus had heard enough and realized that these two lawmen needed to disappear if his plans were to come to fruition. Without thinking any further he said, "that's enough, shoot these bastards."

The three standing regulators hesitated as Willie pointed his cocked shotgun at them. However, Kurt Klaus went for his pistol. Jake made a quick decision and shot him in the foot. Kurt collapsed to the porch screaming as he was cradling his foot.

"I could have killed him for drawing a firearm on a US Marshal. Instead, this is your last chance to cease and desist. The next time he draws on me, he'll die. For now, he needs a doctor since there is detritus of leather and socks in the wound that need to be removed to prevent infection."

Hans turned red-faced and said, "I'll kill you for this!"

"You talk big, have great holdings and money, walk with a swagger, but remember one thing. Your grave's grass won't be any greener than mine and will grow weeds from the shithead underneath."

Jake and Willie stepped up on the buckboard

and rode away after pushing the four bodies onto the ground. A mile down the road, Willie said, "you just hurt two dangerous men's pride. They'll be back in force to get you in time when you least expect it."

"You're partially right, Hans is fuming which may make him act without thinking. However, with declaring him the prime murder suspect, I think he'll lay low for a while till he comes up with a lethal plan that will keep him in the incontestable clear."

"In any event, we need to stay alert and prepare a defense in case of an all-out attack."

***

Back home, Jake went to the chicken coop where Hannah was herding the flock back in the coop for the night's security. Jake looked at Hannah and said, "these birds are following you as if you are the pied piper. How come?"

"Because they are smart birds. I fed them, gave them water and threw seeds in the run. They remember that and will always follow me. They are all healthy hens that will start dropping eggs within days. I hope those flats will be ready soon. Before Mr. Billings left for the day, he said his team would be able to put up the addition tomorrow and the run extension the next day."

"Great, tomorrow we'll go to town and check on the Cass woodshop as well as running many other errands. Most important, we need to be at the train depot at 11AM to receive US Deputy Marshal Clifton Gibson, esquire."

***

CHAPTER 9

HANNAH'S LIMELIGHT

Supper consisted of a chicken pie with all the vegetable fixings, and plenty of coffee with a dessert of jelly filled bearpaws. After cleaning up the dishes, the couple retired to the couch to read. However, Hannah jumped in Jake's arms and another passionate encounter followed.

As things got hot, Hannah pulled back and said, "Jake, I don't know man and I'm anxious about what the future will bring."

"Hannah, what is it that makes you antsy?"

"I don't know if I can respond as a woman should and I don't know what to expect."

"Well, I think it's time to break the ice. Will you trust me?"

"Of course, that will not be difficult since I'm so comfortable being around you."

Jake stood up and pulled Hannah next to him. He then proceeded to slip out of his boots, took off his shirt, unbuckled his belt and unbuttoned his britches. Dropping his pants to the floor, he stood there in his birthday suit. Hannah's eyes went bug-eyed and said, "Oh My!"

"Hannah, there is never shame in nudity between lovers! Now it's your turn. Please undress."

Hannah reacted without hesitation. She quickly undressed and tried to hide her private areas with her hands. Realizing what she was doing, she dropped her hands as Jake took her in his arms. Jake's hands started roaming and touched all her sensitive areas. Hannah was responding and suddenly the inevitable happened.

Hannah's body went stiff, her head pushed back, her eyes rolled upwards as she stood on her toes and her body started shuddering. Suddenly, she yelped and fell limp in Jake's arms. After catching her breath, she whispered, WHAT was that?"

"After years of pent-up urges, that is absolute proof that you are a fully responsive woman, and there should never be any doubt. Now it's your turn to let your hands roam on me. Hannah started slowly but Jake added, "let your hands roam everywhere." When she touched his manhood, Jake knew the inevitable was near. He felt uncontrollable contractions and quickly reached his nirvana. Hannah stood back and said, "and what was THAT?"

"THAT was love juices that make babies."

"OMG, I'm so ignorant!"

"Hannah Bauer, you are far from ignorant. You may not know the ways that humans pleasure themselves, but you're learning. Don't ever forget that you are a self-educated person with an incredible vocabulary. Plus, you are a smart and beautiful woman."

"Can this happen again?"

"Pleasuring ourselves is like a bell, it can ring over and over again."

"Oh Jake, I'm so happy but I'm afraid the balloon will pop, and I'll wake up to find it was all a dream?"

"This is real, we are real." Without warning, Jake gets down on one knee and says, "my darling, I'm so much in love with you, would you marry me?"

Hannah gasped and said, "Yes, Yes, Yes, I'm so much in love with you that it hurts. I want to spend the rest of my life with you."

Jake stood up to kiss her as Hannah stepped aside and came back with a broom. She throws the broom on the floor and says, "it was a custom with my ancestors that jumping the broom while holding hands was a bona-fide marriage when religious representatives were not available. Would you jump the broom with me?"

They jumped together and kissed. Hannah added, "that means we are now allowed to consummate our marriage."

I'd prefer to marry in your Lutheran church. Tomorrow we'll see the reverend and arrange a wedding ceremony in a few days. That will give us time to get you a wedding dress, invite some guests and arrange for a meal at Bessie's for our guests. Now, unless you forgot, we are still naked. Let's get dressed for bed before things progress out of our control, heh."

"That would not be bad, but I'm willing to wait just a few days." That night they fell asleep in their arms. On awakening, Hannah said, "what a night, you were randy all night."

"Uh, is that another word from your books? What is randy?"

"Your manhood was in full tumescence all night."

"If you mean that I was in distress, I agree. Now whose fault was that?"

"I'm glad that I affect you that way. Hey, it's early and we have time to go to the stream for a swim and bathing before Willie arrives for breakfast. Are you game?" "Yes ma'am, but let's bring some clothes in case Willie arrives early."

They slipped on their boots and ran to the stream with a handful of clothes.

Jumping in was refreshing. Before long, they were lathering each other and enjoying every minute. Drying off, they dressed and ran back to the cabin to prepare breakfast. On the way, Jake stopped to water, feed the chickens and pick up the eggs. To Jake's surprise, he picked up eighty eggs and placed them on a bed of straw in a wood box. When he arrived at the cabin, Hannah was pleased to see so many full-size eggs. She then said, "we'll bring them to Herman and start our arrangement. If the flats are ready, we'll transfer them and bring the flat to Herman."

Hannah prepared a large batch of flapjacks as Jake made coffee and set the table. When Willie arrived, they started to eat. After breakfast Willie asked, "what is the agenda for today?"

Hannah said, "the Cass Construction Co. will be building our coop's extension today. With all the banging the hens will go 'henshit.' So, before we leave, we'll move the hens to the run. I normally don't let them out when I'm gone, but today the construction team will keep coyotes away."

Jake then took over. "first, we go back to the ranch to make special arrangements. Then we go to town on business. We'd like your escort to town where you'll be free till 3PM when we'll be heading back to the cabin, and we'll meet at the sheriff's office again."

"Ok, but in case you have unexpected interference, I'll be watching Main street while sitting on the boardwalk."

"Just remember, if we get into a gunfight with regulators, we shoot to maim, not to kill. I would like at least two alive to rat on the killers."

As they were pushing the chickens outside, Hannah was throwing handfuls of corn and oats. Jake added water to the outside water trays and Willie was harnessing the gelding to the new buckboard. As they were about to leave, Elliot Billings arrived with wagons of lumber, tools and six carpenters. Hannah and Jake reviewed the blueprints and left knowing that the foreman would do the job as planned.

Meanwhile at the Circle K Ranch, Hans and Kurt were talking. Hans asked, "who did the shooting at the Sanders' ranch? "It was me and the regulator, Cleo Braun. Grover Bronson froze" "I thought I told you to let the regulators do all the killing." "I had no choice; Sanders pulled a pistol and was about to shoot Grover." "Great, now we have to get rid of Bronson and Braun before they implicate you. Get the last three regulators in here and make sure you don't come in with them. I don't want you to know my plans."

Bronson arrived with Cleo Braun and Slim Rancor. "What do you need, boss?" I want this Marshal Harrison and his bimbo, the Bauer girl, dead." "Do you want us to do it on the trail?" "No, that failed last time. I will give you each $500 to do it in broad daylight, even in front of witnesses. Just barge in a store where they are and shoot them down. To make sure it's done, here is $750 and you'll need to return here for the other $750. I know you three are wanted for murder in New Mexico, so two more killings won't matter. Then I want you to leave the state and I never want to see you again. Do you agree?" The regulators looked at each other and nodded, "Done, give us half and we'll wait in town for them. Just have the other half of the money waiting, because we'll be on the run and not in a mood to wait."

Arriving at his ranch, Willie was sent to the bunkhouse to get Clayton as he and Hannah stepped into the ranch house. "All of this is now mine. It is a well-organized layout. Let me show you around. The main floor has a huge kitchen with dining table, a large parlor with a heating stove, two bedrooms, an office and a water closet. Upstairs are three more bedrooms." After the tour, Willie arrived with Clayton.

"Clayton, this is Hannah Bauer, my fiancé. Willie exploded, "you scoundrel, you never even hinted at the news. Congratulations to you ma'am, you chose a good man." "Willie, my name is Hannah, and Jake chose me, I'm just going along with it." With a huge smile from ear to ear.

Clayton added, "well ma'am, would you agree to meet my cowhands, I'm sure that none of them would recognize you as Miss Bauer. Your transformation is unbelievable." "I'd be glad to, and we'll do that before we leave."

"Now, what did you want boss"

Jake explained the situation with Klaus. "I want two men in the Bauer loft from dusk to dawn. One can alternate sleeping while the other watches. I also want a guard walking the grounds all night at this ranch with one man alternating sleep in the parlor. Each man will be paid an extra $5 for the night shift and you can rotate all your men from day to day. This will continue until the killers are in jail and Hans Klaus is brought under control. Do you anticipate any problems with this plan."

"Not a one, and we'll start the vigil tonight."

"Second, I ordered a manure spreader for your use."

"Third, The Cass Construction Co. will be here in two days to dig a well, install a windmill and inside plumbing. Now, do you have any issues to discuss?"

"Yes, you have almost 1000 head of cattle. I think we need to cull the herd. You have older cows that are barren, too many bulls and several 3-year old steers. If we pull all these, we can bring almost 200 head to the railhead. The price is high this time of year but will crash as winter approaches. Plus, all-natural indicators predict heavy snow this winter. Even with that, we have plenty of hay to support 800 head of cattle plus our remuda. I think we'll get +- $5,000 from the sale and if we do this, now is the time, before we start harvesting our 300 acres of hay, especially if we want to do a second crop before fall."

"That's good planning. Go ahead and do it. Just deposit the money in the ranch account in the Rancher's Bank. Anything else?"

"Just to present your fiancé to the men."

After the presentation, Jake said, "you are all invited to the wedding and reception dinner—at full pay for the day." Hoorahs and whistles followed. As the trio were preparing to depart for town, Hannah had to use the privy. While she was gone, Jake said to Clayton, "would your men extend the small garden space to two acres. Cultivate it and fertilize it with horse manure once the manure spreader arrives; and harrow it again after the manure is on. And keep this quiet, it's a surprise for Hannah." "Will do, right away."

***

The ride to town was uneventful. Hannah found herself wool gathering as she thought of the house tour. Finally, she said, "you have a beautiful house. What was that room off the kitchen?" "That was a scullery—a room with large sinks to wash dishes, pots and pans and even has a sink to do laundry."

"Well, it's a shame to sell the ranch with such a beautiful house."

"We don't have to sell it. We can move in after our honeymoon. I'm adding indoor plumbing for our luxury, you know."

"No, I didn't know. Was that always your master plan?"

"No, but it became utmost in my mind after I fell in love with you."

"Jake, whatever you want or wherever you wish to go, I'll be with you. With that in mind, what do we do with the cabin, land, chicken coop and chickens?"

"We'll hire an older homesteading couple to move in and care for the chickens. Then we'll build you a coop on the ranch, just like the one you now have, and we'll stock it with 200 layers. With 400 hens, we'll supply all of New Braunfels' egg market."

"Wow, I'm no longer obfuscated, and I love your plan, my future husband. By the way, does this master plan include filling all those rooms with children?"

"Yes, if we are fortunate. Obfuscated, huh? Remind me to buy a dictionary at Wolfgang's

Mercantile." Hannah smiled and held onto Jake's arm as they rode along in silence.

Arriving in town, Willie went his way and the Duo went to the Cass office. Cecil came out of his office and said, "we were just talking about you. My shop workers have completed the six flats you requested. Come in the shop to check their work."

The flats were well made. The sides were ½ inch cedar, the bottom was a panel board, the divisions were glued balsa wood with a cedar center board for stability. The cost was $3 per flat. Hannah filled one with wood chips to see how it would work and was satisfied. Jake then ordered twelve more flats. The butchering funnels were also ready and Jake ordered six more. After paying for everything, Jake asked Cecil to go ahead and build a chicken coop and run to match the Bauer coop onto the ranch. Before leaving, Jake left a $700 voucher which Cecil felt would cover all the construction costs. Anticipating a problem in storing the hay from two crops off 300 acres, Jake reserved the construction crew for a hay shed, pending his discussion with Clayton.

Their next stop was the telegraph office where Jake sent a telegram to his parents in Waco. He informed them of his meeting Hannah and invited them to the wedding with the date pending. Their next stop was the post office to check on mail. Jake had a bank statement from his bank in Denver. He looked at the balance and decided that it was time to enlighten Hannah. Hannah took the paper and immediately said, "Jake, this can't be true." Jake nodded yes. Hannah added, "you are a rich man, why are you bothering with cattle, a ranch, the Marshal service, and now an egg business?"

"First, the money will be ours and we'll use it to make our lives easier. But we'll always have business interests to keep us busy. It's part of life and it's going to be our lives." Hannah simply smiled. A quick stop at the Ranchers Bank and Jake made a wire transfer of $10,000 from his Denver account and deposited the bounty vouchers from the dead highwaymen. He also started a benefactor fund with a deposit of $2,000 and made Herman Wolfgang the distributor of funds to his mercantile. Moving outside, Hannah said, "I know, I'll go along with this benefactor account till we get a chance to talk about it, heh?"

Their last stop before meeting Clifton Gibson was to set him up with a room in Mrs. Sanborn's boarding house, located next to the courthouse.

As Clifton stepped onto the platform, he immediately saw Jake standing next to a beautiful blonde. "Hello Marshal, and who is this lovely lady?"

"This is my fiancé, Hannah Bauer, and you'll be coming to our wedding. For now, let's get some dinner (that's lunch in Denver) and I'll bring you up to snuff on this mess."

After ordering a ground beef burger with home-fries and coffee, Jake gave a detailed chronological description of everything that happened since he came to New Braunfels—excluding his love life. As their food arrived, the subject changed to a more social level. After dinner Clifton summarized his plans.

"The first thing I'll do is to prepare the prosecution of the three attempted rapists. The second is the malfeasance and obstruction of justice charge against the sheriff and prosecutor. The third is to start investigating the Klaus clan at the Circle K, the presumed guilty murderers of your family and several homesteaders. Is that it for now?"

"Yes, and Judge Aiken will be more than happy to work with you. Your office is next door to the judge and your housing and meals is at the Sanborn boarding house. Last, wear your pistol, you never know what the Klaus clan can do. If you need protection, I have a deputy by the name of Willie Irving, who will be available to you. Plus, Sheriff Herb Bixby will also be a willing and capable asset to help you."

After escorting Clifton to the boarding house, the Duo went to the Lutheran church to speak to Reverend Ernest Schaefer. This being early June, there were several weddings ahead, but a firm date was established in seven days at 11AM.

Their next step was to set up a reception dinner at noon on the wedding day. When asked how many guests were planned, the Duo started writing down a list: Herman and Helga Wolfgang, Herbert Heinz and wife (hardware), Frank Werner (livery), Sheriff Bixby, Judge Aiken and wife, Clifton Gibson, Clayton Briggs, Willie Irving, Cecil Cass and Elliot Billings (construction), Adelbert Bromley (freighting), twelve ranch cowhands (cook included), and Jake's parents (Amos and Erna).

"Hannah answered, "make it for at least 30 +-5."

Their next stop was the newspaper office where they had 40 wedding invitations printed. The cost included delivery, to all the invited guests, by the regular newspaper delivery boy.

Their last stop was the Wolfgang Mercantile. On entering Helga noticed Hannah's huge smile and knew what was coming. Jake was holding a 6-dozen flat full of eggs. Herman could not believe his fortune. Jake said, "don't pay us for each delivery, keep a tab and give the delivery person a receipt. We'll settle later and your next delivery is in two days."

Helga asked, "so what's new with you two?"

Hannah beamed and out loud said, "we're getting married," as Helga took her in a celebratory hug. Herman was quick to add, "congratulations you two, you've both made a great choice."

"Thanks, now we need to get dressed for the occasion, Hannah needs a wedding dress and accessories and I need a coat, vest, white shirt, dress pants and a Texas shoelace necktie."

Herman said, "fine, Hannah you go with Helga and I'll take care of Jake." In no time Jake was fitted with a dark gray coat and Hannah had several boxes of clothing that Jake was not to see till the wedding.

"The next thing we need are wedding bands. As Hannah made the choice, Jake saw a ring with a bright white rock. "What is that?"

"That is an engagement diamond, rather expensive at $170."

Jake picks it up and puts on Hannah's ring finger. "We'll take it, since by Hannah's facial expression, we would need to take her finger off to get the ring back!" "Oh Jake, it's too expensive!"

"Do you like it?" "Why of course!"

"Then display it proudly, because I certainly am proud to see it on your finger—it's one of the great signs of commitment on both our parts, heh?" As Hannah plants a very passionate kiss on her future husband. Reality was restored with Helga clearing her throat.

Jake pocketed the wedding bands and says, "the next item on our list is a dictionary." Herman adds, "I see Jake that you are learning new words from Hannah's reading!"

"Yes, but moving along, my dad will be my best man, but would you consider walking Hannah down the aisle?"

"Oh lord, I always had a spot in my heart for your fiancé, and I would be honored with the privilege of giving her away."

"Great, for the next item, we are looking for a resident couple to take over the Bauer cabin, garden and chicken coop/egg factory as quick as by our wedding day in seven days."

"Of all the homesteaders who sold out east of here to the Circle K, there are three left in town. They have all banked the meeker amounts they got for their farms and are hoping they can repurchase them again in the future if things change with Klaus. Two have young families and one couple is childless at the ages of 50. That last couple is Karl and Ida Newmann. Karl works as custodian at Billy Joe's saloon and Ida is a chambermaid in the Zimmerman Hotel. These are great people with strong religious and work ethics. You would do very well to get them."

"We'll go see them today. The last item is this, and this is news to Hannah. Since I'm putting roots in town with my marriage, ranch and chicken farm, I want to introduce you to a Benefactor Fund. I have been fortunate as a bounty hunter to amass a small fortune, and I wish to share some of my wealth with those who are having a tough time paying their mercantile bills. For anyone who has over $30 in overdue payments, and are worthy of some help, pay their balance off but don't tell them who is paying. I wish to stay anonymous. I have started a special bank account at the Ranchers Bank, and you are authorized to make withdrawals."

"Oh my, that can run you into serious money. I already have fifteen customers who fit that bill—worth well over $450."

"That's OK Herman, the Benefactor Fund has $2,000. When the balance gets below $200, let me know."

As they stepped out and loaded their boxes onto the buckboard, Hannah said, "I was still wondering if you were ready to set roots down. But now I know and I'm so happy. When we have a chance, we need to talk about your being a US Marshal, for now we'll just go along with it, heh?"

Jake thought, *"hu'um, getting back some of my own medicine. This woman is getting to be a real handful—it's going to be a wild ride with very few dull days. I knew Hannah would be my equal."*

Arriving at Billy Joe's, Jake recognized the bartender, Sam Cooper. Before Jake could speak, Sam said, "I was just about to send someone to your ranch with some crucial information. Last night, three regulators showed up and did some heavy drinking. I heard them say that they were paid to kill you and Miss Bauer. Having received half their pay, they decided to get out of town and head out to Austin, being 50 miles from town, to enjoy drinking, saloon girls and gambling. Now if you ask me, in two weeks, they'll be out of money and be back here to collect the other half of their arrangement with you know who?"

"Got it. Now I would like to speak to Karl Newmann."

"Just left to go home, he lives at 79 Pearle Street Unit #3."

Jake dropped a $20 gold double eagle on the counter and thanked Sam for the information. Stepping outside, Willie was sitting on a chair next to the batwing doors. "What brings you here, Willie?"

"Watching you go from one merchant to another is ok, but when you head to a saloon, that perks my senses up. In this case, I heard what Sam said. Looks like things will come to a head in two weeks."

"Yup, right after our honeymoon in San Antonio."

Riding the buckboard to Pearle Street,

Hannah said, "what's this about a honeymoon in San Antonio?" "Just go along with it for now, it's supposed to be a surprise!"

Knocking on unit #3, the door opened, and Ida said, "yes, what can I do for you?" Hannah said, "we'd like to hire you." After a long explanation, Jake finally said, "you would move into the furnished cabin, take care of the garden and chickens and deliver the eggs to merchants in town. We'd like you to move in the day of our wedding in seven days. You would have sole control of the chicken farm. Your pay would include: $30 per month, all vegetables and eggs you can eat, one butchered chicken for meat twice per month, a shotgun and shells to keep coyotes at bay, all the firewood you need and I'll even add a parlor or bedroom heating stove for winter comfort. You only need to provide your other food, clothing and personal items."

"Also included is a harness horse with a new buckboard for farm business, egg delivery and personal use. You'll be on the account at Heinz's to buy the supplies needed to maintain the chicken/egg enterprise."

Hannah then took over. "To make your transition easier, we'll give you a moving fee of $40 to help fill the cabin larder and whatever else you need. If you accept, we'd like you to come to our wedding. It would alert the merchants of your new position with us and you'd get to meet our ranch hands. Remember one thing, if ever you need help and we are not available, you can always rely on our ranch foreman, Clayton Briggs, and his cowhands. You will never be alone."

Ida was seen wringing her hands and finally said, "Oh Karl, this is an opportunity of a lifetime for us. It's better than ever getting our homestead back."

Karl stood up and said, "It would be our pleasure and we'll treat your chickens like they were our own. We're not going to let you down." Everyone shook hands and Jake handed gave Karl $40 as promised. Karl added, "we'll give our weeks' notice and will be around some night this week for a review of your methods and general orientation."

"Do you have a horse?" "No, we'll walk."

Hannah said, "nonsense, Willie or we'll pick you up at 5:30PM in two nights." Karl said, "whose Willie?"

Jake said, "that black man who is always following us. He's also a US Deputy Marshal and a great friend of ours. You'll always be able to trust him."

With their business taken cared of, they made their way home to spend a week on the chicken farm and develop a system that was as efficient as possible. During the week, they would also supervise the ranch's plumbing and construction of a new chicken coop. The week would culminate in their nuptials.

***

CHAPTER 10

ESTABLISHING TWO ENTERPRISES

Arriving home, Elliot was loading his wagons with his men and tools. The extra lumber was stacked in the carriage house and Elliot invited Jake and Hannah to check out the new extension. As Hannah walked in, she said, "Oh my, look at the shelves, work area, hand pump well and storage for straw and wood chips. It's perfect."

Jake thanked the men and gave them all a $3 tip to reflect his gratitude. Elliot added, "tomorrow we start with the well, windmill and indoor plumbing at your ranch. Cecil said you may want a chicken coop as well, have you decided?"

"Yes, can you duplicate this coop and run?

"Certainly can. The water/plumbing team will do their job, and this carpenter team can start tomorrow on the coop and run. Just put your stakes where you want the coop. Do you want a pump well?

"No, instead run some cold-water pipes from the house."

"Good choice. See you at the ranch and thanks for the men's tips. That was a nice touch!"

For the next week, they busied themselves with the daily routine of caring for the chickens. The first morning, they gathered 6 dozen of eggs. It was clear that the new flock was adjusting to their new home and ready for laying. Every day they fed and watered the chickens. Jake ground up a turnip and realized that the smell would contaminate the coop. So, he used some leftover lumber and built a 20-foot trough outside to feed the ground up vegetables.

During the noon dinner, Jake asked, "do you have a Montgomery Ward catalog?" "Yes, pa bought the latest issue." Jake started investigating and suddenly said, "here it is."

Hannah looked over his shoulder and said, "what is that machine?"

"It says it's a defeathering machine. After the usual scalding dips in 145-212° water, with one turn of the wheel, these flexible fingers rotate five times. The feathers are all pulled out and if you keep the chicken in the bowl too long, the skin will start coming off. We need this when we butcher, instead of using manpower to pull out feathers."

Hannah exclaimed, "nice, we need to buy two, heh. I see it also says that the left-over young feathers are burned off over a wood fire, just like we now do."

That evening Willie picked up the Newmanns. They were very pleased to see the cabin and agreed where the heating stove would be installed. They went to the barn to check out the harness, gelding, the new buckboard, straw, wood shavings, chicken feed and oyster shells. The chicken coop was the longest portion of the tour. Jake explained how the vegetable grinder worked and how to feed the ground up vegetables in the outside trough. Hannah explained how much and when to feed the chickens.

The Newmanns were encouraged to pick up the eggs twice a day and to not pick up wooden eggs. Karl laughed and agreed it was a good idea to use wooden eggs. Jake said that he had ordered two extra dozen from the Cass woodshop.

They then went to the garden and encouraged Ida to keep up the plantings by purchasing seedlings at the hardware store. They pointed out that chickens like ground up cabbage, turnip, carrots, beets, sugar beets, corn, potatoes and squash for pecking. They gave them the list of foods to avoid. Also, they were informed to plant any other vegetables they liked to eat, and all seeds and seedlings were paid thru the farm account. After the tour, and an extra hour answering questions, the Newmans were comfortable with the arrangement and assured Hannah that they would move in two days before the wedding since their employers were willing to let them go early.

The next morning, Willie showed up for

breakfast to get his orders for the day. Jake said, "we have to deliver some eggs and have business at Heinz's Hardware and the Cass woodshop." "I'll ride with you to town and back. Then, Clayton wants me to go hunting for coyotes that are threatening young calves. I'll be back tomorrow morning as usual, if that's ok?"

Hannah cleaned the dishes, Jake collected 12 dozen eggs and prepared three flats as Willie harnessed the gelding to the buckboard. As they were about to load the three egg flats, Hannah said, "whoa, those eggs are not all placed properly. In each slot, the large end of the egg needs to be up. The pointed end needs to be at the bottom since it is the strongest part of the shell. The large end up allows the air pocket to be up and this keeps the yolk in the center of the egg for protection. I'll remind the Newmanns to do the same." A rearrangement followed.

The Trio arrived in town without issues. Willie sat outside the establishments and waited. The first three stops were the three mercantiles that received each a flat of eggs. At Heinz's

Hardware, they ordered two defeathering machines, all the water and mash feeders for the new coop and added the usual straw, wood shavings, mash, layer pellets, buckets and oyster shells—and arranged for Bromley Freighting to deliver them to the ranch barn. They ordered the usual mix of 200 nine-month-old layers to be delivered one week after the wedding when Jake and Hannah were moving in the ranch. The last item was seedlings. Jake had to admit that he had asked Clayton to cultivate and fertilize a new garden site at the ranch. So, Hannah happily picked up all the seedlings that Heinz had on hand and chose many bags of seeds. Hannah added, "looks like our work is cut out for this afternoon, we're planting all these seedlings and seeds to get our garden started."

Their next stop was the Cass woodshop. The workers had finished six more flats and 24 wooden eggs. The lathe worker explained how he turned a hardwood block on the lathe and produced an egg in record time. He explained why the ends were squared off. The block of wood was secured at both ends in the lathe vices and finally cut off in the band saw. Hannah was pleased and added, "the cut off ends will make the identification between real eggs much easier."

To meet the needs of the second coop, they ordered more wooden eggs, flats and butchering funnels. Before leaving they settled the construction and woodshop account with Cecil. Finished their business, they added some dry goods and fresh beef and returned to the ranch to start planting their garden. After a quick snack, they moved the seedlings to the new garden.

Hannah was amazed to see the new garden. The soil had been fertilized and harrowed to a fine finish. In addition, the crow-wings had formed perfect raised rows ready for planting. Clayton showed up and said, "I assumed that this is what you wanted, since I went to your homestead and spied how your garden was laid out and I duplicated it."

"This is perfect, thank you."

"I see you have several hundred seedlings

ready to plant. I can spare three men if you want some help?"

"Hell yes! Jake and the cowhands can plant the seedlings and I'll put in the seeds." "And I'll help you with the seeds. We'll have this garden planted before supper time."

By supper time, Jake and Hannah were back at the homestead. They did the chicken chores, picked up the eggs and secured the chickens in the coop for the night. After feeding and caring for the horse, they went to the cabin and started preparing their meal of baked potatoes, boiled carrots, biscuits, beef steaks and coffee. For dessert they had a blueberry pie form Wolfgang's Mercantile.

After supper, they went back to reading. Jake was reading his book on the care of chickens when suddenly he asked, "if chickens don't pee, how do they get rid of kidney waste? And even more perplexing, if chickens have only one hole, why is it that the eggs are not covered with poop?"

"For the first issue, chickens don't make liquid urine. Their kidneys put out a powder called urate crystals. The chicken's feces are blue/green but the white coating on the droppings is the urate crystals."

"Now the second issue is a bit more complicated. The feces and eggs do exit from the same hole, which is properly called the 'vent.' When the egg comes down the oviduct, it falls in a structure called the cloaca which turns inside-out so the egg cannot come in contact with feces."

"Boy, you are some smarty! What am I going to do with a wife that knows so much?"

"You're going to make love to me like you did a few days ago when I was a poorly informed hayseed. Now kiss me and whatever!"

As the passion was rising, Hannah said, "in a few days we won't have to stop. For now, we'd better hold off since I'm getting pretty close to you know what."

"Ok, but let me assure you that once we're married, my 'tally wacker' won't be randy all night." "I think you mean 'taily-wagger,' to signify the dog's wagging tail." "I don't mean dog, I mean MY 'tally-wacker,' my lady." As they both started laughing out loud.

Despite Jake's distress throughout the night, they made it to morning in time to prepare breakfast before Willie arrived.

***

The Trio was having a breakfast of oatmeal, toasted bread and coffee when the hoofbeats of an incoming rider was heard. Willie got up to look out of the window and said, "it's the telegraph messenger." Willie gave the boy two bits and handed the message to Jake. After reading the message, he said, "it's from prosecutor Gibson. There is a hearing at 10 o'clock today, in lieu of a trial, for the three accused attempted rapists and Hannah and I are needed to testify."

As usual, Hannah picked up the kitchen, Willie saddled the two riding horses instead of the buckboard, and Jake watered and fed the brood. Hannah arrived at the coop and gathered 12 dozen eggs and stored them in two flats. With the chickens left in the coop, the Trio headed to town.

Arriving in town, the trio noticed that the main street housing the merchants was a mess with horse manure everywhere. Jake would mention this to the sheriff. Once inside the courthouse, they were directed to Judge Aiken's office where Clifton Gibson was waiting with the judge. The judge started, "thank you for coming with so little notice. As you noticed, the streets are a mess and I have a proposal. Our street sweeper broke his leg on the job and will be out of work for the next six weeks. We've advertised the job, but there are no takers. I am proposing that the three miscreants be offered the job in lieu of a prison sentence at Huntsville Penitentiary. How do you feel about this Miss Bauer, since you're the victim, and your attackers would still be in town."

"I'm not a vindictive person but I firmly believe that some public comeuppance is needed for their behavior. If you're willing to substitute prison time for community service, then I agree with you. As far as those men remaining in town, they still can come back to town after serving their term. To me, if they show some remorse, I say it's Ok. How do you feel about it, Jake?"

"If it's Ok with you, it's Ok with me!"

"Mr. Gibson, what say you?"

"Since this is all my idea, I agree and thank you for considering the proposal."

When Sheriff Bixby arrived with the prisoners, he was invited into Judge Aiken's office. "Tell me sheriff how the three accused are behaving?"

"When they were thrown in the hoosegow, they were angry, and every other word was a threat of revenge. Now, after ten days, they have done an about face. I guess they know they're heading to Huntsville where they will be raped as they were going to do to Hannah. The three really look miserable and I believe they would like to apologize to Hannah."

The prisoners were brought in and the judge started, "since you have waved your rights to a trial, I'm now prepared to pass sentences. By state law, I am allowed the maximum sentence of one year in prison in Huntsville."

One of the accused broke down and started crying. The other two were stoic and nodded their heads in resignation. The judge continued, "however instead of this prison sentence, let me make you an offer. Our street sweeper is out with a broken leg. We need street sweepers, for the next six weeks, to clean up the horse manure in our streets. Were you to accept, you would clean up the manure using the town manure spreader and spread its loads onto a neighboring farmer's fields. During the six-week period you may sleep in the jail's open cells, get two full meals a day, a mid-day snack, be free to walk the streets without entering a saloon, and have your clothes laundered each day. In addition, in the evenings, were you willing to empty the merchant's privies, the merchants would pay you $1 for each privy you clean out. You could end up with a nice stake to restart your lives. What say you?"

The three accused looked at each other and each nodded with a smile. "We'd be happy to accept your generous offer, including the offer to clean out the public privies. Thank you, and we'd like to apologize to Miss Bauer."

Hannah said, "I accept your apology, and good luck with this second chance."

After leaving the courthouse, Jake brought them to the wagon factory. In the show room was a new buckboard similar to the one they had recently purchased. Jake asked, "assuming this is for sale, how much will it set us back?" "Same as the last one." Jake gave him a bank draft and asked where they could buy a harnessed horse.

The salesman said, "Frank Werner told me that he had purchased a fine harnessed gelding yesterday from an army Captain who had confiscated him from bootleggers. He apparently got him at a fair price and has already sold the wagon the horse came with. The horse is still for sale." "Fine, set the buckboard outside and attach the item I have on order."

Heading for the livery, Hannah said, "wow, that's a fine buckboard I can use on the ranch. What is this item you're talking about?"

"That's a surprise, for now go along with it, heh?"

Walking in the livery, Hannah immediately spotted the gelding. She walked up to him, offered him a sugar cube and rubbed his head as the horse nickered. Frank stepped up and said, "he's a gentle one and the harness is included. He luckily cost me only $50."

"Will you take $75."

"No, but for a regular customer, I'll take $60."

Willie brought the harnessed gelding to the wagon factory and attached him to the new buckboard. The salesman then presented Hannah with a paper wrapped package. As she unwrapped it, she exclaimed, "OMG as she turned it for Willie to see, EGG LADY. The salesman affixed the sign to the hooks on the tailgate as the trio headed for the ranch.

Passing by Heinz's Hardware, Willie stopped the buckboard and said, "I talked to Elliot this morning and he told me that the coop would be ready by tomorrow. If you're willing to have Mr. Heinz order your chickens, I'd be happy to care for them until you return from your honeymoon."

Hannah never hesitated, "fine, let me go inside and put in our order as well as arrange for their delivery along with the feed and other supplies."

Arriving at the ranch, Clayton met them and arranged for a cowhand to care for the new gelding and park the buckboard in the carriage house.

The duo walked to the chicken coop and were amazed what six carpenters had accomplished. The frame was up, and the roof was half done. The plumbing team had the windmill pump up and were laying pipes to the coop's extension. As they entered the ranch house, three plumbers were piping the kitchen, scullery and water closet.

After their inspection tour, Jake asked Clayton, "how are things going with the hay harvest. I see the baler is busy putting out some nice bales."

"Things are going very well with good weather. However, with all the manure we've added, the first crop is yielding more hay than we had anticipated. I'm afraid the barn loft will be filled with the first crop and without more storage, we'll have to abandon the idea of a second crop."

"I prefer you harvest a second crop. I'll have

the Cass carpenters build an addition to the barn to store the second crop—if it's Ok with you?"

"That's great, if we end up with a surplus, we'll have no trouble selling it to nearby ranchers, homesteaders or even city folks."

"Done. Now I have an idea I need your opinion on. What do you know about crossbreeds?"

"Funny you should ask; George Sanders had researched the subject and was convinced that crossbreeds were the future of the beef industry. Breeding the Texas Longhorns with polled Herefords and Durham short-horns yields animals that are more resistant to disease, calve easier, yield more weight on the hoof, handle winter month better, and seem to thrive on the Texas range. The problem he faced was the lack of supply. These breeds come from England and bulls can run into $40-$60 a head—if you can find them for sale."

"How many bulls should we have to start a crossbreed program?"

"Since we culled the heard, we made an inventory. You have about 900 head that are spread out as: 500 cows and heifers of breed-able age, 200 calves, 100 heifers, 100 steers and 30 bulls. On the average, it takes one bull to handle 10-15 cows. According to George, it was not clear if the insemination rate might go up with the Hereford and Durham bulls, or whether the calving survival rate would be higher. In any event, it appears that the ratio of breed-able cows to calves would improve."

"Would you be satisfied to change the makeup of the herd?"

"Yes, but I doubt that you can find a supplier for 30 bulls."

"If I were able to find a source, what would you do with the Texas Longhorn bulls we now have"

"I don't think we should ever place all our eggs in one basket. Were you able to purchase 15 bulls of each breed, I think we should keep at least 5 mature Longhorn bulls. If the new breeds take hold, we'd get rid of the Longhorn bulls the second year. This way, the 25 bulls we bring to market will help pay for the Hereford and Durham stock."

"Do you happen to know who has such breeds?"

"The only ranch I know of is the Circle P Ranch west of San Antonio, owned by a man called Emmitt Powell."

Jake's eyebrows went up when he heard the name. "Thanks for the information, I'll get back to you on this. In the meantime, after the first harvest, go ahead and select the 5 bulls you want to keep and segregate the other bulls for now. If I can't make a deal with Powell, we'll still have a full count of bulls for the fall breeding season."

That evening after supper, Jake and Hannah had a long talk about changing the herd. Jake pointed out that they still had five days before the wedding, and Jake's parents were not arriving for three days. Jake could take the train to San Antonio and be back the same day. Hannah had too many things to see to before the wedding and would stay. It was agreed that Willie would spend the day with her as her security.

The next morning, Jake was at the railroad office getting a free two-way ticket with Duseldorf's card. Because of the card, the agent sent a telegraph to the San Antonio office requesting Emmitt Powell meet him at the railroad office for an important personal business meeting, c/o US Marshal Jake Harrison.

An hour later, the train covered the 30 miles as Jake arrived in San Antonio. Jake disembarked and was pleased to see an old face.

"Well, I never thought we would ever meet again. What on earth brings you to San Antonio?"

"Bulls, I mean Hereford and Durham bulls!"

"Well, in that case, let's hit my favorite diner and talk over breakfast."

Jake started by providing a detailed sequence of events since his bounty hunting days to the present situation in New Braunfels. Emmitt then clarified his present status, "when you returned my stolen funds, I might have not clarified what the money was for. I had purchased a large herd of Hereford and Durham bulls and cows. I was given three years to pay the English investors or lose my ranch. That was the biggest gamble of my life and you saved my bacon by returning my life's savings. I made the payment that day and returned to San Antonio. That was about a year ago and this fall, I plan to start selling breeding stock. So, your arrival is certainly uncanny."

"I assume that you have been raising crossbreeds during these three years, are you satisfied with the result?"

"Better than I ever hoped for. My buyers have seen the crossbreeds and they want my purebred bulls. The bidding and offers are getting out of hand. So, tell me what you're after."

"I'm looking for 20 Hereford and 20 Durham bulls as well as 20 Hereford and 20 Durham breed-able heifers. This would allow me to crossbreed my Longhorns and also maintain a purebred line of Hereford and Durham animals

"The current high bid is $60 a head for bulls and $30 a head for breed-able heifers, can you match that?"

"I can do better. By the time you start selling, the bids will likely be higher. So, I'll offer you $65 and $35 a head. If my math correct that comes to $4,000. Here's a bank draft off my account in the Ranchers Bank of New Braunfels."

"Marshal Harrison, you have a deal. The 80 head of cattle will be on a train in three days."

***

Jake got back on the train and when he arrived in New Braunfels he found an entourage waiting for him. Present were Hannah, Willie, and Clayton. Hannah gave Jake a welcome home kiss and then everyone wanted to know if he had been successful.

"Yes, in three days by train, we're getting 80 head of purebred stock to include 20 Hereford bulls and 20 heifers, and 20 Durham bulls and 20 heifers." Clayton added, "that's even better. We'll separate the paddocks so we can breed the purebreds with their kind and still have more bulls than needed to breed the herd of Longhorns."

Arriving at the ranch, Jake was amazed to see the finishing touches to the coop. After the men finished, they left their tools in the barn and planned to return in the AM with loads of lumber to start on the hay shed and another wagon with posts and chicken wire for the run. The plumbers would be back in the

AM with the coal burner, a load of coal and enough lumber to build a separate enclosure for the boiler.

With things under control, the Duo returned to the cabin for supper. After cleaning up, Jake said, "time to do the finances for the egg enterprise. My computation is based on six mercantiles receiving our eggs and two chicken coops full of layers. Take one coop of 200 chickens. If each hen lays 3-4 eggs per week, that comes to +-700 eggs per week or +-60 dozen. Assuming the three mercantiles can handle 3 dozen per day or +-20 dozen per week equals again +-60 dozen."

"So, 60 dozen eggs is the magic number per week. At 30 cents per dozen, that comes to $18 per week or +-$925 per year. Now add +-$75 per year for the sale of poultry meat and deduct 65cents per day for feed, oyster shells, vegetable seedlings/seeds, wood shavings and straw. The expenses come up to +- $250 per year and the income is +-$1,000. Now the net profit is roughly $750 per year for a couple hours work per day."

"The reason I presented this is to show that

two operations can generate $1,500, but minus the Newmann's salary. Yet you're still working only 2 hours per day and making a wage of +-$1,100 per year, which is three times the current hourly living wage of $1 per day. I'd say that's not bad for a hobby business. Plus, that leaves many hours for another activity—the potential for which I'm beginning to recognize."

Hannah admitted, "it's more than a hobby, it's stress management and a labor of love. I feel a connection to those birds and it's hard to explain. I guess I just enjoy the entire enterprise. Now what is this 'other activity' you're alluding to?"

"Time will tell, just go along with it for now, heh."

***

The next morning, they bathed at the swimming hole followed by the morning ablutions. At breakfast, realizing they had four days left before the wedding, they decided to make a schedule of activities they wanted to do and left room for things that would happen out of their control.

The first day Clayton and his cowhands were busy separating three paddocks. The largest was to house all the bulls till breeding season in the fall. That way, calving was delayed till warm spring weather. They also built two small paddocks to breed the Hereford and Durham heifers come fall. The 25 longhorn bulls were herded to the train railhead in preparation for the new stock.

The Duo went to town to deliver egg flats. They also made arrangements with a butcher and two late evening convenience stores for the same egg delivery as with the Wolfgang, Fischer and Lehmann mercantiles. The Newmann's would handle the three new additions.

That first night, the subject of maintaining a US Marshal status came up. Jake was first to admit that he didn't know what Captain Ennis would do, but Jake wanted the ranch, the chicken farm, a wife and family. The US Marshal badge was second in the running.

It was Hannah who said, "Jake, you have a natural instinct for living and survival skills. Unlike bounty hunting, as a US Marshal you can always have a backup. It's not that I don't want you home every day and night, but I accept that you have a duty to perform and I know you will do it safely with honor. I guess it all depends on what the Captain has planned." Jake added, "after the wedding, we'll likely have to travel to Denver and have a serious chat with him."

The second day the Cass plumbers came to show the Duo how to fire the wood boiler and maintain continuous pressure in both the cold and hot lines. Later, they installed a heating stove in the Bauer cabin.

That afternoon, the laying hens arrived. As before, the hens were delivered to the prepared coop. Hannah watered them till they drank their fill and fed them some chicken mash. To introduce them to the run, she opened the door and shooed them outside. By supper time, the flock was pushed back in the coop to perch for the night and possibly lay some eggs. Hannah was again leading them around like a pied piper. Jake finally asked, "what is the name of the sounds these birds make?"

"The everyday sound is called 'clucking.'

When scared, as by coyotes, they produce a high pitch 'screech' that you can't miss. The third and interesting sound that chickens make is a 'crow' sound that they make as they pass an egg."

The third day, Wyllie and the telegraph messenger hand delivered the wedding invitations. The Duo went to the ranch to finish planting the garden with the recently arrived new batch of seedlings. While there, they saw that the hay shed was coming along nicely. Hannah pointed out how the center of the shed had a drive thru to avoid backing up a horse drawn wagon full of hay bales.

At the end of the day, was moving time. Willie moved to the bunkhouse, the Newmanns moved into the cabin and the duo moved in the ranch house.

By 4PM the duo was heading to town to meet Jake's parents at the train station. Arriving, Clayton met them and asked them to come to the stock yard to see the new herd of bulls. "You said you had purchased 80 head, but the stockman shows 84. There seems to be four extra funny looking bulls. What are they?"

Jakes looks at the herd and says, "I'll be darned, those are crossbreed bulls, two were crossed between longhorns and Herefords and two were crossed with Durham Shorthorns."

"Hum, maybe this enclosed note explains the mix-up."

Jake opens the note and starts laughing as he reads, "to an honest man who, instead of absconding, brought back the robbed bank's $20,000 of which $10,000 was my money. You saved my life's dream and now enjoy yours."

Walking over to the passenger platform, the train from Waco had covered the 150 miles in five hours. As the Harrisons stepped on the platform, Erna walked right up to Hannah and gave her the biggest hug possible. Erna said, "thank you for capturing my son's heart and getting him to settle down." It was obvious that the ladies were happy with their initial encounter.

"Welcome dad, you still sheriff or you close to retirement?"

"My lead deputy is now taking over, and I'm basically doing desk duty. I expect to be fully retired in a few months."

Jake escorted his parents to Zimmerman's Hotel where their stay had been prepaid. "Rest and freshen up and we'll meet in the hotel restaurant at 4PM. We have a lot of catching up to do."

The Duo then went to see Reverend Schaefer for the pre wedding practice. Herman was already at the church as well as the reverend's wife, the organist. The reverend put them thru the paces till they all knew their positions and responses. When the wedding party left, their anxieties were resolved, and they were ready for their life's event.

Supper with the senior Harrisons started as a walk thru memory lane. Eventually Amos asked the serious question, "now that you have decided to settle down with a wife, cattle ranch and chicken farm, what are you going to do with your US Marshal status?"

Hannah interjected, "I'm not marrying your son to change him. We hope that Captain Ennis has a solution to the problem, since I fully accept the fact that Jake is a natural lawman and will always continue in some capacity—hopefully in the New Braunfels area."

"Well, I happen to know that the issue is soon to be resolved, for now just go along with it, heh."

Hannah looked at Jake and said, "now I know where that aggravating phrase comes from."

After supper, the Harrisons were brought to the ranch for a tour.

Leaving their horses at Werner's livery, Jake rented a two-seat buggy from Frank and headed east. Their first stop was at Hannah's homestead. There they met the Newmanns and walked thru the cabin, barn and chicken coop. Amos was mostly interested in the chicken coop and its layout as well as the great looking brood of hens. Their second stop was the ranch. Erna was totally enthralled with the running water in the kitchen, the boiler, the water closet and the massive ranch house with the extra six rooms beyond the kitchen and parlor. She finally commented, "if you plan to fill all these rooms with children, you're going to be mighty busy." Hannah answered, "no, just three of them."

After seeing the duplicated chicken coop with a full explanation of the process of collecting and delivering eggs, the Harrisons were more than impressed. Hearing Jake's plan to develop a cross breeding program, Amos added, "now that is a novel idea that I look forward to see." It was then Erna who shocked everyone as she said, "well Amos, don't you think it is time to fess up?"

Amos wavered and finally said, "Erna has never asked much of me during my years as sheriff. Now that my retirement is close, she has asked me to move from Waco and move closer to you two. She feels that we need to be next to our only family. We are prepared to sell our house and buy one in town or build one closer to you."

Hannah exploded, "then why don't we build you a small house and barn next to us. Wouldn't you want to be close to your grandchildren? I know I'd love to have you next door."

Amos smiled and added, "yes, we would love

that. Besides, I wouldn't mind helping out with the egg enterprise, hay harvest, or cattle ranch to keep busy. Erna added, "and I would like to help take care of that huge garden you are growing as well as babysitting your babies."

Jake never missed a step. "Then it's settled, tomorrow I'll go with you to see Cecil Cass to design a house, barn, windmill well and indoor plumbing. We'll start construction as soon as we return from our honeymoon."

And so, the next day, the wedding preparations began in earnest.

***

CHAPTER 11

PREPARING FOR THE FUTURE

The wedding day preparation turned out a real surprise when Erna arrived at 10AM and informed Jake that he had to be dressed in his suit and out of the house by noon. Hannah's preparation would then start, and she'd be ready for the 4PM wedding. Jake asked, "why does she need four hours to get to the church?"

"Because she needs to bathe, style her hair, dress, find something old, something borrowed, and something blue. And you cannot see your bride until she walks down the aisle. Now get dressed and scat. Go spend some time with your dad in town and be at the church on time."

There was no arguing with his mom and Hannah had a huge smile as she added, "guess for now you're going to have to go with it, heh?" Jake proceeded to comply and quickly made his exit. They headed to Bessie's Diner for a noon meal. They managed to drag the afternoon away at Billie Joe's, by talking about old times, his years as a bounty hunter and Marshal Service year. When the subject of money came up to build a new house, Amos was wondering if the sale of their house in Waco would cover the building price of $1,000 as proposed by Cass Construction. Jake resolved the issue by telling his dad what his bank account balance was and assured him that the cost of their new home would be a retirement gift. The sale of the Waco house and their life's savings would be their retirement nest egg. Jake made it clear that the only thing that mattered was their involvement in their lives.

By 3:30, Jake and Amos made their way to the church. Jake was waiting with his dad at the front of the church as the guests started to arrive. With some 35 guests, the church pews were well occupied. The last apparent guest was Jake's mom escorted by Sheriff Bixby. Strangely enough, Erna moved over from the edge of the front pew to make room for someone else. Suddenly, to Jake's surprise, entered Captain and Mrs. Ennis as they proceeded to Erna's pew. Amos then whispered to Jake, "that's what I meant when I said to go with it for now."

A lull in the ceremony seemed to occur till Reverend Schaefer stepped up and moved next to Jake. With dead silence and without warning, the organist pounced on the organ and started playing Wagner's Bridal Chorus. As Hannah and Herman appeared at the church doors, a soloist began with 'here comes the bride………"

Jake nearly melted away as he saw Hannah in her white dress. As Hannah started walking down the aisle, arm in arm with Herman, Jake whispered to his dad, "OMG, that's the most beautiful woman in the world, she simply looks effervescent." When Herman released her, Jake and Hannah took each other's hands and fortunately Reverend Schaefer took over the ceremony because both participants were frozen in mutual thoughts. Eventually, Jake and Hannah heard the words, "and as a representative of the state of Texas and God, I now pronounce you man and wife—you may now kiss the bride."

After the kiss, the guests erupted in applause as the bride and groom made their way to the back of the church. There they stayed and greeted their guests as they exited the church. The last guest to exit was Captain Ennis who said, "we'll talk sometime today." The bride and groom then made their way outside with hoots and hollers as well as handfuls of rice and confetti over their heads. The Reverend then invited all the guests to Bessie's Diner for a reception and supper.

Bessie had announced all week that the diner would be closed on Friday evening for a private party. In actuality, after the noon dinner, the diner closed, and all the cooks and waitresses spent the afternoon decorating the entire diner. They had set up a table of honor with name plates to include Mr. and Mrs. Amos Harrison, Reverend and Mrs. Schaefer, Mr. and Mrs.

Hermann Wolfgang and of course Mr. and Mrs. Jake Harrison.

Before the meal, Sam Cooper, of Billy Joes saloon, was handing out free beer or fruit punch. People were milling about and talking. Jake was pleased to see the Newmanns talking to the ranch cowhands as he and Hannah moved about trying to visit with everyone. One of the last to get Jake and Hannah's attention was Captain Ennis.

"Let me just start by saying that I received two invitations to your nuptials, your dad and Clifton Gibson. I guess they saw something happening that would affect you and the Marshal Service. So, before I begin, how do you feel about Jake's situation?" Hannah answered, "it's a no brainer, I love this man and whatever he decides, I'll support him 100%. I've already told his dad that Jake was a natural lawman and should continue in some capacity as a concurrent husband and rancher."

"Ok, well this is my offer. Texas is being divided in different federal districts. The Southeast district extends from Waco to San

Antonio and includes the Rio Grande Valley. That's almost 200 square miles, all accessible by train, and all under the control of one Federal Judge located in New Braunfels—Judge Harland Hobart, an old friend."

Hannah asked who Judge Hobart was. Jake answered, "a judge that I rescued from assassins holding guns on him, and who tried to hire me as his personal bodyguard."

"The actual offer is to be in charge of the district with three assigned deputies. You would still be able to manage your ranch and assign Judge Hobart's processes. You would be needed on manhunts and other serious assignments. Think it over for a month and then get back to me."

Without warning, Bessie was pounding a spoon on the back of a cooking pot to get everyone's attention. "For the menu tonight, I couldn't bring myself to prepare a chicken or beef dinner seeing the bride and groom own a chicken farm and cattle ranch. So, I have prepared two main courses. You have a choice of fresh roasted turkey and stuffing or fresh pork roast. All with fresh buttered rolls, mashed or baked potatoes with plenty of vegetable sides. There's plenty of food and seconds will be welcomed. Also, save room for dessert—apple or blueberry pie with ice cream and coffee. Enjoy your meal courtesy of Mr. and Mrs. Jake Harrison."

Each guest made their choices and food was individually served. The leftovers were added to the tables, family style, for self-serving. Drinks included the leftover beer, fruit punch, as well as milk, water, tea and coffee.

The tradition of hitting a spoon against an empty water glass was started by Erna of all people and was widely grasped by the cowhands. Yet the bride and groom were pleased to acknowledge the clanging glass with a kiss. When the guests realized that the bride and groom were more than eager to cooperate, the clanging seemed to quiet down.

The reception dinner started winding down and by 8PM, Jake and Hannah were making their way to the train station with several large cases. They were taking the one-hour train ride to San Antonio for a week's honeymoon and stay at the Grand Canfield Hotel and Restaurant. Hannah was experiencing several new things: a train ride, seeing a city, staying in an elegant hotel and having a husband.

***

The short train ride to San Antonio was a sacrifice for the newlyweds. Simply holding hands became foreplay for what was waiting them. Arriving on schedule, the Duo took a taxi to their hotel. The hotel porter greeted them and secured their luggage. The registration was quick since the reservation for one of their two bridal suites had been made by telegraph. Once inside their suite, the porter explained the three rooms: parlor with lounging chairs and table, bedroom and water closet/bathtub with running hot and cold water. Before departing he added, "if you need meals, drinks or chambermaid services, simply pull this cord and a bellman will respond to your door for your order." As he left, Jake gave him a $1 tip.

As soon as the door was closed and locked,

the newlywed's passion exploded in a lustful demonstration. The clothes went flying as well as any possible inhibitions. After consummating their marriage, Hannah said, "OMG, when my passion peaked, I thought I was going to lose my mind. Is it always going to be like this?"

"I can only say that I'll do my best to make it happen. Now let's try again, but this time let's make it last longer. That first time was our lust, now let's slowly pleasure ourselves to show our love."

The first night passed with very little sleep. In the morning, after some quick ablutions, the duo was again at it. Afterwards, Jake said that he needed a replenishing breakfast to restore his energy. Jake said, "would you pull the cord and order a full breakfast. Hannah looked under the sheets and said, "Jake Harrison, have you no shame, you're randy again!"

"Well, whose fault is that, heh?"

Hannah put a robe on and got up to pull the cord. Jake suggested, "can you close the top of your robe with a safety pin or broach, your breasts are spilling over. If you don't do something, the bellman will be fighting with the waiters, as to who will deliver our tray. I don't want you to be the envy of the hotel staff."

"Well, I don't know that a bit of envy is bad."

"That may be true, but my eyes will be the only ones to know what is under that robe." Hannah just smiled in satisfaction and after affixing a broach, pulled the cord.

The second day of their honeymoon was spent in the room, and mostly in bed. By supper time. Jake suggested they dine in the hotel's restaurant followed by a Shakespeare play in the theatre. Hannah agreed especially since she had read all the Shakespearean plays and had never been in a theatre. The meal started off with an appetizer of escargots and the main entrée was prime rib au jus with asparagus, roasted potatoes and a burgundy wine. Dessert was a caramel flambé with tea and coffee. After finishing this elegant fine supper, Hannah agreed that it also served as a replenishing source of energy.

The theatre's production that evening was Romeo and Juliette. Even if Hannah had read it several times, she was totally mesmerized by the fine details, costumes and actors' abilities. Jake spent as much time looking at his wife's profile as he did looking at the stage. He then realized that his wife had missed a significant bit of culture. After the presentation, Jake asked Hannah what she thought. "At first, I didn't want to lose one evening in our marital bed, but you knew better. I'm so shocked at the culture I missed growing up, that as a one-year anniversary present, I would like to come back to San Antonio and visit the theatre again."

"We will do that, but for the rest of the week, lets visit the different theatres nightly."

That night, their sleep had intimate interruptions, but they managed to get more sleep and by 11AM, they made their way to a diner for a late replenishing breakfast of steak and eggs. Afterwards, Hannah asked what Jake had in mind for their 3rd day agenda. "I thought I would drop you off at a garment store for you to purchase evening dresses for the theatre, dresses for home, riding skirts and under garments, as well as picking out a new suit for me. Take your time and I'll be back later to try the suit on after I check out the new firearms in a city gun shop. Remember, buy what you want since I don't know when we'll be back to the city and we'll ship everything by train."

After dropping Hannah off, Jake was on a mission. He walked in Wyler's shop and found what he was looking for. By the time he had all the accessories, repair kit, maintenance kit, a "how to" manual, a backup reference, and registration fee; his bill came to $149. Jake arranged for everything to be packed in four boxes and shipped by train to his ranch in New Braunfels—all for Hannah's surprise of her life.

Getting back to the garment store, Hannah had seven large boxes already chosen and packed for shipping. When Jake reminded her that they were going to the theatre, she pilfered two boxes out of the bunch for evening ware. He then tried on his new three-piece suit with a white shirt, a derby hat and new boots. His items were all packed in an extra box and all boxes were added to a railroad crate where they would stay till their departure. His bill came to $178 which he paid with a bank draft.

316 | Richard M Beloin MD

After their shopping spree, they had time to get back to their room for baths. Their supper turned out to be a new event. Jake added, "this is not a replenishing meal, it is a romantic dinner, the first of many we will have. The menu consisted of a tenderloin shish-ka-bob, twice baked potatoes and a medley of roasted vegetables with a pink Chablis wine. After two hours of private conversation over a gourmet meal, the two headed out to a romantic play in current times. The newlyweds did not need any more motivation, yet the ambience was feeding their appetite. At the end of the production, Jake said, "I'm hungry, feed me."

Hannah looked at Jake and said, "Jake, we just had a full supper, how can you be hungry?"

"Woman, I'm not hungry for food, I hunger for you. I guess, I just can't get enough of you."

"In that case, let's go to our room and you can get as much of me as you want, but save some for the future, heh?"

The fourth day started with another replenishing breakfast of corned beef hash, poached eggs and home fries. After several cups of coffee, the newlyweds went for a walk on Main Street. Their first stop was a photography shop. They had photographs taken as a couple and as individuals. The shop provided different costumes and they had photos taken as cowboys, their present dress, and elegant theatre attire. The photos would be ready in three days and so they paid for shipping to their ranch.

The next stop was a bookstore. Hannah managed to buy six novels and a new Webster's dictionary, as Jake bought a textbook on crossbreeding Texas Longhorns and one book on drilling for oil and how to market crude oil.

Their last stop was an agricultural implement store. The salesman quickly volunteered to give them a tour of the new implements. The duo saw more than they understood, but fortunately brochures were available on every piece of machinery. They collected all the brochures to give to Clayton, as the salesman emphasized that Heinz's hardware store could order any of these implements thru a telegraph order to Winslow Agricultural Implements here in San

Antonio—the only distributor in Texas with the parent company in Denver Colorado.

That evening, after another romantic dinner of pork tenderloins with brown rice, boiled broccoli and white wine, the newlyweds went to the theatre to see a musical play. To Jake, this type of show was an improvement over a Shakespeare or romantic play. To Hannah, it was another pleasing cultural event.

The fifth day was touring day. After another replenishing breakfast of pancakes, syrup, sausage, and coffee, the newlyweds visited a renowned historical museum on San Antonio. Afterwards, they took a taxi to visit the historical Alamo. The tour was well prepared and rendered with the highest patriotic respect possible.

Approaching the hotel, Jake saw a furniture store and had the taxi driver drop them off. "Let's go inside to see what furniture we might want to add to our new ranch house." They entered and toured the show room of incredible displays. As they walked about with the assistance of a salesman, Hannah was making a mental list. Getting to the end of the show room, the newlyweds sat down with the salesman. Jake was asked to present the pieces he was interested in.

"We need extra chairs for large parties or meetings. I liked those folding hardwood chairs which appeared sturdy and were storable in a closet. Now we have three bedrooms on the ground floor. The master bedroom is adjacent to a small room which would serve as a nursery. The other large room should be split in two with an adjoining door and a door to the outside. You would have an office next to the nursery and I would have an office next to the porch but adjoining yours. I would have Cass build me an elbow high counter and a door to the porch. This would be my office to be shared with Clayton. That means I need a two ended desk, filing cabinet, and closed-door cabinets. You keep the present furniture for your office. I also want two of those newly designed stuffed recliners for our parlor with a table between them. Last, we need a lockable gunrack in my office."

Hannah was next to add to the list. "We should have a braided rug in the parlor and each bed should have nightstands. I also would like a sideboard with drawers for the kitchen and a hutch for the dining room."

With their order complete, they retired to the salesman's office for a tally:

- 12 folding chairs--$24
- Office desk--$20
- Office filing cabinet--$20
- Office cabinets--$10
- 2 stuffed recliners--$40
- Table between recliners--$5
- Gunrack--$10
- Braided rug--$20
- Kitchen sideboard--$20
- Dining room hutch--$30
- 8 nightstands--$16

Total	$215
Shipping by train	$22
Local freight to ranch	$12
Grand Total	$249

Jake paid with a bank draft and then added, "I suppose you'll want to fill the sideboard and hutch with fine porcelain dishes, clear water glasses and sterling silver eating utensils, heh?"

"Why yes, but in due time. I have to check our bank account and prices on Montgomery Ward catalog before enduring this type of expense."

That evening, with another romantic dinner of glazed duck, potatoes au-gratin, and fried zucchini squash, they then took a taxi to the theatre to see a comical play. After finally catching their breaths, Jake said, "when we get stressed with work, we'll take a train ride to the city, have a romantic dinner and stay at the Grand Canfield Hotel. We'll watch a comedy and get to rewind ourselves for another stint in New Braunfels."

Hannah was pleased to say, "that sounds so wonderful."

That evening, a sense of reality came back. The newlyweds talked about Jake maintaining his US Marshal status and taking Captain Ennis' offer. Hannah said, "I knew the instant the Captain made you that offer that this was meant for you. With Clayton running the ranch, you'll be free to follow your duty. BUT, with backup deputies, or I'll be coming along with my shotgun and Bulldog—that's not negotiable. I've finally found a loving husband and I'm not letting any outlaw take him away."

Jake jumped on Hannah and smothered her with kisses. Before they knew it, they were back in the sack. Now finally getting a full night sleep, Hannah woke up and said, "I think the honeymoon is over, since I slept all night, heh?"

Jake agreed, "Yes, it's time to go back. Let's pack up, and make our way to the train station, buy a return ticket and telegraph Willie that we are returning home today. We'll ask him to meet us at 1PM at the train platform with the buckboard to haul our packages."

***

Arriving back home, Willie was waiting for them. "I have some bad news. Those three regulators are back in town as Sam Cooper had predicted."

"That is fine. We have business at the bank and town clerk, and we'll spend the night at the ranch. We'll be back in the morning to confront these three killers and take some alive. We need at least one to implicate Klaus and his son, two would be even better."

At the Rancher's Bank, the teller said, "nice to see you're back, folks. Mr. Wolfgang asked me to remind you that your Benefactor Account is down to $426."

"Very good, transfer $2,000 out of my account. Now, I would like to add my wife to my account and change the account's name to Harrison's ranch and egg farm." After the papers were all prepared, the teller handed a form for Hannah to sign. As she applied the pen to paper, she noticed the account's balance. "Jake, I think there is an error of an extra zero." The teller looked at the amount and said, "no Mrs. Harrison, the account balance is just over $100,000."

Jake added, "just apply your signature to it dear, and go with it for now. I'll explain later."

Walking to the town clerk's office, Hannah said, "I'm waiting, dear!"

"I had a successful year as a bounty hunter and when I entered Lawman School I had almost $90,000 in the bank. As a US Marshal, I amassed another large amount of bounty rewards. Since my arrival in town, we collected on the three-highway man who tried to kill us, plus Clayton culled the herd for cash. Despite all my expenses with construction, wages, and buying a herd of bulls, I still have a sizeable nest egg. That's why I keep saying to buy whatever you want."

"But Jake, you have enough money to never have to work a day for the rest of your life, certainly not to work at a dangerous lawman's job."

"Well actually, you're just as rich as I am. Do you want to sit on your money and not have a reason to get out of bed and enjoy life?"

"Touché. I don't want to change a thing either. Heck, I'm going to be the richest chicken farmer selling eggs at 30 cents a dozen!"

Arriving at the town clerk's office, Jake asked that Hannah be added to his deed and for himself to be added to Hannah's deed—but maintain separate deeds for legal purposes. After the paperwork was done and copies were given, Jake asked to change the brand of the original Sander's ranch. "The new brand will be the Circle H, and the branding iron will look like a 'H in a circle.'"

After their business was done, the three rode back to the ranch. They were on extreme alert since the threat of an ambush was high. Yet, the ride was uneventful. Arriving home, Willie helped to unload the buckboard, unharnessed the horse to the barn, and then went to the bunkhouse for dinner.

Walking to the porch, Jake picked up his wife and walked her over the front door's threshold. When he let Hannah down, they both saw four boxes on the dining table. Hannah said, "what did you do, buy me a present. I didn't need any more than you to make me happy."

"Hannah, I know that you have a secret love."

"Jake Harrison, I'm mortified, you know I don't have a secret lover! You're the love of my life and that will never change."

"I didn't say secret LOVER, I said secret LOVE. Just open this box labeled #1, which will be self-explanatory."

Hannah opened the box and gasped as she stood back and spotted a typewriter. "How on earth did you know, can you read my mind?"

"Well a little bit, but not to this extent. Since we consummated our marriage and made love regularly, you started talking in your sleep as you entered in a relaxed sleep state. At first, the occasional words like introduction, contents, page count, chapter one and the like didn't mean much. When you blurted your first full sentence, I knew what you were hiding."

"What was the sentence?"

"It was, "Jake, I want to write my first book!""

"But Jake, it's only a fantasy, my life is with you."

"No, it's more than a fantasy, I know you're capable of writing and you are fortunate to have writing as a hobby. This will be something you can go back to any or every day, and still have a life handling the chicken farm, the cattle ranch and me."

Hannah couldn't hold back any longer, her tears reflected the pride she had in her husband. Finally, she got some words out and said, "I only hope I can unselfishly encourage you as you have done with me today."

"Now let's go over each box individually. This typewriter is the latest model put out by Royal. It has its own keyboard and replaceable printing ribbon with many other features that are too much for me to remember. Your enclosed operator's manual will explain these"

"This second box has many accessories to include: 12 replaceable ribbons, ribbon ink, a maintenance kit, a repair kit, pencils, a fountain pen with ink, erasers to use on dry typed ink, 9X12 binders, clipboards, carbon paper, and the very important manual of how to type, where to place your fingers and which finger activates which letter etc. etc. etc."

This third box is four packs of 8.5X11 inch typing paper. Each pack has 500 sheets. The last box is the current Encyclopedia Britannica which will be your reference source. Last but not least, open this envelope."

Hannah was again on the verge of tears as she opened the envelope. "Jake, what is this, I don't understand."

"My darling wife, I am sending you to college. In our town, on School Street, we have a branch of San Antonio's School of Writing. I have registered you for a course called 'Authorship 101.' It is a beginner course that emphasizes composition, grammar, punctuation, sentence formation, paragraph content and chapter orientation, and of course typing. The current trend is for an author to type the story as it's forming in his or her mind—no more handwritten manuscripts. It was suggested, that you learn how to place your fingers and which finger activates what letter before you come to class. This typing course emphasizes familiarity with the machine and accurate speed typing."

"How will we find time to go to class each week?"

"We'll make time and we'll manage. Class is held two days a week from 3—5PM on Tuesdays and Fridays. You'll go to class and I'll run errands. After class we'll have dinner at Bessie's and then come home. Now this is a commitment on your part, you need to study the assignments and practice speed typing. You have to type 50 correct words a minute to pass the course."

That evening after supper, the couple unloaded their garment boxes and luggage. The office furniture was moved to Hannah's side of the room. The typewriter was place in the center of the desk and accessories were added to the closed shelves or filing cabinet. The separating wall and connecting door would be next to be added.

After their intimate encounter, Jake said, "now watch what you say in your sleep if you want to keep some secrets."

"No matter what I say, I'll never have another secret to hide from you. Just don't listen to my babbling—that's all."

***

The next morning after a replenishing breakfast with Willie, they prepared their firearms. All three were armed with their pistols to not show extra armaments in town.

They wanted to look like they were in town to conduct business. On arrival, the Trio went to the Cass Construction Company. Jake arranged for Elliot to build a separating wall with door, an elbow high counter and a separate door to the porch. After arrangements were complete, Willie saw the three outlaws walking across the street, "here they come boss."

Jake insisted that Cecil leave the office because of an impending gunfight. Cecil didn't hesitate as he walked over to his woodshop. The Trio positioned themselves with their back to the customer counter and facing the front door. Hannah was told to unholster her Bulldog and hold it at her side. Suddenly the door busted open and three pistol-toting killers stood in obvious surprise. The leader said, "what the hell, how come you were expecting us. Well it don't matter, we've got you under the gun and you're all dead."

Jake spoke up, "we're US Marshals and you're all under arrest for threatening federal officers."

"Those are big words for idiots with their pistols holstered."

"Wrong, my wife has her pistol in her hand."

"So what, never seen a woman amount to much muster in a gun fight."

At that moment, the leader pulled back his hammer as Jake realized it was again time to kill or be killed. Jake knew the only way to stop a bullet coming their way was to shoot the leader in the brain or the groin. The brain shock would paralyze the shooter's reflexes. As Jake drew and fired, Willie drew and shot the second outlaw in his shooting arm's shoulder. Hannah quickly shot the third man in the belly and shot him a second time when he stood there holding his pistol at Jake.

After the smoke cleared, Jake said to Willie, "help me load the two injured regulators on the buckboard and as I head to Doc Craven's City Hospital, go fetch Sheriff Bixby, prosecutor Gibson and Judge Aiken. Tell them to bring some legal documents to write and record a deathbed statement, and a possible statement to implicate a murderer and turn state's evidence."

At the hospital, Doc Craven had attended to the man shot in the gut first. His name was Cleo Braun and Doc Craven said that the gunshot wounds would be eventually fatal. He was about to offer the victim some laudanum when the full entourage of law officials arrived. Jake took over and asked Doc Craven to hold off the laudanum for a few minutes as he addressed the outlaw.

"Cleo, the doc says it's pretty bad and you're not going to live. Since you're going to meet your maker, you may consider clearing your conscience and tell us who sent you to kill us and who killed Rose and George Sanders. If you choose to do so, after your statement, the doc will give you laudanum, a pain killer to ease your departure. If you have nothing to say, you're still going to get the laudanum."

"Yes, I would like to make a deathbed statement. It was Hans Klaus who sent us today to kill Marshal Harrison and his wife. Also, I was in the party that executed the Sanders couple. Kurt Klaus shot George Sanders in the back and I shot Rose Sanders in the head. Grover Bronson was there but never pulled his gun out of the holster. So help me God!"

As Cleo was making his statement, attorney Gibson was inking his words to an official document. Afterwards, Judge Aiken reread the statement and verified that Cleo understood the words without changes. After Cleo Braun signed his name, his signature was witnessed by Jake, Sheriff Bixby and attorney Gibson. Other witnesses to sign was Hannah, Willie and even Judge Aiken.

After a therapeutic dose of laudanum was administered, Clifton asked Grover Bronson if he would admit to Klaus sending him on this mission to kill the Marshal as well as the mission to kill the Sanders. Clifton made it clear that a guilty verdict could be negotiated to a prison sentence, instead of a hanging, if he turned state's evidence. Grover didn't even hesitate as he said, "quickly write it up before the doc puts me under with ether. I'll sign it."

It was then that Judge Aiken was signing his name to a document. He then handed it to Jake, "here is an arrest warrant for Hans and Kurt Klaus. Good work you all. Finally, overdue justice will reign."

***

CHAPTER 12

JUSTICE AND THE FUTURE

The Trio stopped at the ranch to get their riding horses, rifles, and shotguns as they then headed to the Klaus ranch. Standing on the access road and looking at the gate sign with the big Circle K sign, Jake commented how stupid some humans can be. To throw their entire lives away because of greed.

Pausing for a moment of silence, Jake then presented Willie's job as well as Hannah's function on this important arrest. He reminded both that they were not to put their lives in danger to save outlaws. Moving to the ranch house, the team stepped down without being invited to do so. As they were securing the horses' reins to the railing, Kurt Klaus appeared on the porch and yelled out, "you're 'persona non grata' on this ranch. So, get back on your horse and get the hell out of here before my cowhands shoot you down."

Jake answered, "Mr. Klaus, are you addled or are you just like a bad penny, you keep showing up with threats. Well, here's my answer. You're under arrest for the murder of George Sanders." At the same time, Hans Klaus was seen walking from the bunkhouse with nine well healed cowboys. "I heard you, but you're not taking Kurt anywhere."

Jake came back and said, "I'm taking you and your son into custody. Kurt is being charged for murder and you are being charged with ordering several murders and attempted murders."

Klaus wasn't wavering. He instructed his cowhands to get ready to shoot the lawmen. Jake quickly said, "I have two shotguns on you men, if you start going for your guns, four loads of OO Buckshot will be coming your way and most of you will die. This is not your fight, so be wise and stand down, this is your only warning and it's time to decide."

Klaus saw his men hesitating and added, "stay with me and it's worth a $500 bonus for each man." The apparent foreman said, "we're cow punchers, not gunfighters. What good is the money when we're dead." The leader walked away as did the other eight cowhands.

Seeing that Kurt was going to hang, he went for his gun as Hans yelled, "No-oh-oh." Willie responded quickly and turned his shotgun on Kurt and fired. The impact caught Kurt in the chest and pushed him into the wall where his body bounced back and went flying off the porch onto the ground, face first, at Hans' feet.

As Willie applied the manacles to Hans' wrists, Jake added, "Mr. Klaus you are a pathetic ogre. Because of your greed for oil, you have lost your son and this ranch. You'll now go to prison for life if the judge doesn't hang you."

Klaus growled these words, "I doubt it. Mark my words, I'm way ahead of you. I'll fight you and your law with a fancy lawyer from San Antonio, and I'll get off. Then I'll send assassins and you'll all meet a violent end. That will be my revenge."

***

The trial started three days later. The morning was spent by Judge Aiken doing the actual "voir dire" and after only an hour he had his jury of twelve men. The judge was mostly concerned with choosing jurors who were not friends with the accused or were not biased in rendering a verdict. The prosecuting and defense attorneys had nothing to say in the choosing of jurors.

The trial started with both attorneys giving their opening remarks. Clifton emphasized that he would present witnesses to Klaus' crimes. The defense attorney, Jorg Shultz from San Antonio emphasized he would be discrediting the witnesses.

The prosecutor presented his case by starting with a deathbed statement from Cleo Braun. After reading the statement, he was about to ask the witnesses to testify when Shultz objected.

"I object to the introduction of a deathbed

statement especially one witnessed by lawmen, a doctor, a woman and a judge."

"Overruled for lack of basis, proceed Mr. Gibson."

After having each witness attest to the legal validity of the dying Cleo Braun, Clifton presented Grover Bronson. When Grover clearly admitted that Hans Klaus had sent him along the Sanders' execution as well as the attempted murder of Jake, Wyllie and Hannah, Shults again objected.

"I object to a lying criminal who puts blame in order to negotiate a lighter sentence."

"Overruled, it's perfectly acceptable for any outlaw to accept a lighter sentence for turning state's evidence, and you know that, Sir."

When Clifton tendered the witness and closed his case, Shultz presented a pointless, vague, and confusing set of questions. The defense attorney's witnesses included two ranchers who would attest to Hans Klaus' gentle non-violent nature. The spectators started to guffaw when the judge's gavel came down with threats of emptying the room. To everyone's surprise, Shultz closed his case and never called the lawmen to the witness stand for cross examination.

Seeing what Shultz had done, Clifton said to Jake, "oh boy, we're in trouble. No defense attorney behaves this way unless they have an ace in the hole."

After closing arguments were given, the judge gave his instructions to the jury. "Take your time, deliberate without bias, and come back only with a unanimous verdict."

An hour passed and no verdict. A second hour passed, and the bailiff announced that the jury foreman wanted to ask the judge a question.

"Your honor, we have deliberated for hours, voted many times but we are deadlocked."

"What is your present voting result?"

"Eleven for a guilty verdict and one against."

"Very well, go back to the jury room and continue deliberating. If the vote doesn't change in 2 hours, come back to the courtroom and I will need to call a mistrial."

The judge then invited the attorneys to his chambers. The judge simply asked, "what in blazes is going on." Shultz simply shrugged his shoulders as if lost. Clifton said, "Jake said that Klaus's last words were 'mark my words, I'm way ahead of you.' I believe that Klaus has bought a juror and the jury will remain hung."

The judge thought a bit and finally said, "I believe you're right Mr. Gibson. I recollect signing a bank forfeiture months ago against one of jurors, once we know the holdout's name, we can check the man's bank account by court order. Even seeing a large deposit will not help since you would still be hard pressed to prosecute him for jury tampering. I think we will now be dealing with a mistrial. So how would you two attorneys wish to proceed."

Shultz immediately jumped in and requested a change of venue. However, Clifton refused to accept this, and the idea was rejected by Judge Aiken. Clifton suggested an immediate retrial to prevent Klaus from arranging another fiasco. The judge agreed. Shultz objected but was told by the judge that his defense would be the same. So, the case would be retried tomorrow.

Clifton then added, "this time I suggest that

the 'voir dire' be conducted by Shultz and I. Shultz said, "why?"

"So, I can question potential jurors on their finances!"

"Your honor, I object because ah, ah. ah!"

"Overruled, as usual you don't know why you're objecting." The judge added, "I will let you attorneys do the 'voir dire' and will allow you each three 'preemptory challenges' and an unlimited 'challenge for cause.'"

Returning to the courtroom, two hours later, the entire jury came back to the courtroom. The foreman admitted they were still frozen with the same 11:1 vote. The judge declared a mistrial and shocked the spectators when he announced the retrial would start tomorrow morning. Hans Klaus was obviously disturbed and was speaking way too loud to Shultz as Hannah heard him say, "that's not enough time to get another man on board." "Sorry but it's out of my control, you should have anticipated this could happen. Now it's my defense or nothing."

***

The retrial started at 8AM. Clifton started the "voir dire" with a rancher. "Sir, do you have a mortgage on your ranch?" "I thought that line of questioning was private." "It is except I have the right to ask you since you are applying for a seat on the jury." "Ok, yes I do." "Are you current on your mortgage payments?" "Yes I am." "Are you a social friend or business friend of Hans Klaus?" "No, I just know of him." Clifton said to the judge that he accepted the man for a spot on the jury. Shultz only question was in the line of bias against German people. When the answer was no, Shultz accepted the juror.

The selection seemed to progress smoothly since the potential jurors had accepted the line of the attorney's questioning. After selecting five jurors, a man was on the stand. When asked if he was late in making his mortgage payments, the potential juror admitted to being eight months late. When asked how he was planning to catch up, the man said it was none of anyone's business. Clifton said, "your honor, I wish to exercise my first preemptory challenge and reject this potential juror without a reason."

Shultz objected but Judge Aiken almost stood up and yelled, "Mr. Shultz, don't you know the law, you cannot object to a preemptory challenge, it is the other attorney's prerogative."

Later, Shultz used a "challenge for cause" when a man clearly hated German people and was denied a spot on the jury because of a bias cause. As the jury selection continued, Clifton used all three of his "preemptory challenges" and two of his "challenge for cause."

Shultz had difficulty in deciding how to best use his challenges and before he knew it, the twelfth juror was accepted and the "voir dire" ended. Since it was now noon, the court recessed for dinner and would resume at 2PM.

During dinner at Bessie's Diner, Hannah said, "I know the 'voir dire' is over but would you explain the difference between a 'preemptory challenge' and a 'challenge for cause.'" Clifton answered, "the 'preemptory challenge' is an objection to a proposed juror made without the need to give a reason. Whereas, the 'challenge for cause' requires that a reason be given why a juror would not be able to judge without a bias."

By 2PM, the opening statements were given, and Clifton presented the same witnesses. The only difference was the defending attorney's performance. Shultz had become an aggressive and confrontational lawyer fighting desperately for his client. Clifton said to Jake, "Shultz is fighting like the 'devil fell in holy water.' This change in Shultz's behavior signifies that they don't have an ace in the hole. The way he is pressuring and threatening my witnesses is Klaus' only defense, but it won't be enough."

By 4PM the attorneys were ready for their closing statements. That is when Klaus went berserk. He could clearly be heard at the prosecutor's table, "you don't have enough defense, you need to bring more witnesses." "But Hans, there is no one else to testify on your behalf, even your own cowhands refused to testify."

As usual, the judge gave his instructions to the jury and again explained that he expected a unanimous verdict and stated they were to deliberate till they reached this level of certainty.

With the jury out, Jake suggested they all

go to Bessie's Diner for supper. Clifton said, "unless I missed all the clues, I think the jury will be back by the end of an hour. Let's wait."

On the five o'clock chime, the bailiff, Sheriff Bixby, announced that the jury had reached a verdict. Sitting in the jury box, the foreman stood. "Mr. foreman, have you reached a unanimous verdict?" "Yes, we have your honor." "What say you." "Guilty as charged." The judge then polled each juror to confirm the 12:0 count in favor of a guilty verdict. The judge then announced a two-hour break for supper and declared that the court would reconvene at 7PM for sentencing. Shultz objected. "Your honor, I need a few days to gather character witnesses in order to plead 'mercy on the court.'"

Judge Aiken loudly declared, DENIED, see you all at 7PM as the gavel came down and the judge headed for his chambers.

At the diner, there was some rejoicing. Hannah expressed the feelings of many when she said, "justice has finally arrived and maybe we can finally live in peace again." Clifton then asked what Jake thought about the two choices—a hanging vs. a prison sentence. Jake was honest and said, "hanging is the only way to end this man's hold over the community. With a prison sentence, this man will find a way to divert funds and hire assassins to deliver his revenge—and some of us will succumb."

Clifton added, "well, let's hope that Judge Aiken can see that and sentence the man appropriately."

On time, Sheriff Bixby called the court back to order and for all to stand. With the judge at his bench, Sheriff Bixby instructed all to sit. Judge Aiken started, "The defendant will stand. Mr. Hans Klaus, your reign of tyranny will now come to an end. You are an evil man who has no respect for the law or human life. Unfortunately, your kind never changes, and you will always be a threat to mankind. For this reason, a prison sentence is not justice, and so I sentence you to hang tomorrow morning at 8AM. Court is adjourned." As the gavel comes down, the judge turns to walk away.

"Your honor, I object to the immediate sentence, we plan to appeal."

The judge returns to the bench and says, "denied. In view of the mistrial caused by Mr. Klaus' jury tampering, the appeals process will automatically be denied. The sentence stands."

Klaus collapsed in his chair and had to be carried back to the jail. The next morning, Hans Klaus was executed on schedule. The entire legal team was present as Hannah recognized an old classmate. Jake saw her looking at the man and asked, "who is that man?" "That is Dieter Klaus, estranged but legally adopted son of Hans Klaus. The likely heir of the Circle K Ranch and our new neighbor, heh!"

***

A week later, the office renovations were completed, and Jake met with Clayton in his new office. "Well, things have been happening, so let's talk about the hay crop results and the cross breeding."

"Thanks to great weather and motivated cowhands, we filled the new hay shed with a perfect second crop. Even with a bad winter, we'll have a surplus and stand to make a nice profit. Honestly, I think we should cultivate another 100 acres and plant a fall crop of oats. Next spring we'll harrow the field and plant the usual local grasses for hay. The straw can be used feeding inactive horses during winter months and it can also be used in the laying boxes. If we have a surplus of oat feed, we'll have no problem selling it. What do you think?"

"What a fantastic idea. What do you need to make this happen?"

"We'll need a large commercial manure spreader to haul the chicken manure from your cabin and we'll need to start looking for horse manure from other non-crop ranches. It's also time to buy a fertilizer spreader and start buying some granular phosphate fertilizer."

"What about extra harvesting implements"

"To process oats, we'll need a thresher with a winnower. It's also time to extend the baling concrete platform and buy a second baler."

"With this growth, I'll have Cass build us another hay shed, but this time it will be twice the size to accommodate future growth."

"I have to admit, I almost screwed up when

Elliot built the hay shed. He insisted that they add a wood floor. Apparently, we would have lost the first layer of bales to mildew and rot if stored on dirt."

"Ok, we'll include a wood floor. I'm very happy to see this growth, but it seems to me we're going to need more employees."

"Without a doubt. However, I think it's time to have two crews. The herd will get bigger and the crop business will have more demands. I would like to have designated cowpunchers and crop farmers. I've checked around and there are many homesteaders that have sons ready to work off the homestead. These young men are eager, have experience with agricultural implements, and there are many within a few miles west of town that can travel daily and not overload our bunkhouse. These workers would be seasonal from spring to fall and employment would be dictated by need. During peak harvest, the cowpunchers will be available to help as they have done in the past."

"Agree 100%. Go ahead and start hiring. Let's get them involved with the proposed 100 acres this fall. Lastly, how about you, what are your personal plans."

"Well I plan to marry soon, and my fiancé wants to get involved with crop farming as her parents are now doing on a small scale. The problem is finding housing that is close to the ranch."

"Are you willing to stay with me for the next five years?"

"Without a doubt, you have my word."

"How much am I paying you now?"

"$70 a month with room and board.

"Let me make you an offer. I will build you a house and barn a quarter of a mile east of the ranch. To support a wife and household, I will double your salary and if your wife wants to work crops, hire her. You will now become the general manager and you will need to designate two foremen to handle crops and cattle. You'll have complete control of the enterprise since as a US Marshal, I will need to be away at times."

"Wow, that is more than generous, I can only say thank you and I accept. I guarantee you my total loyalty."

"Great, now let's talk about the crossbreeding program." "The breeding season started June 1st. Normally, it runs six weeks but this year, it will be finished by July 1st. The three breeds of bulls, Hereford/Durham/Crossbreed are extremely active and are leaving the six Longhorn bulls in the dust. The cowhands were surprised to see the mating capability of such short-legged bulls. The selected Hereford and Durhan heifers were all bred and were added to the general herd."

"As I recall, we have 500 cows and heifers that were in breed-able age. Any idea on the % insemination?"

"I think it will be very high because we saw only 20% of cows/heifers come into heat the second time within the first month. We only saw a rare cow/heifer coming into heat the third time and none the fourth cycle."

"Excellent, now with the harvest done what do the cowhands do?"

"Well, they will be working on cultivating, fertilizing and seeding those 100 acres along with the new homesteading kids. Plus, I want to do a mid-summer herd culling. Those six

Longhorn bulls can go. We also have one Hereford and one Durham bull that is not interested in mating. We've marked both of these with ear cuttings and they need to go. We also missed some older barren cows on the last culling, and they can go. We have a dozen cows who lost their calf from failing to thrive. The vet calls this a genetic defect and strongly suggests we pull the cows out of the herd. Last, we have a half dozen three-year-old steers that are troublemakers. They fight with cows and other bulls and worse of all, they keep breaking thru the barbwire fences. They certainly have to go because they're too much high maintenance."

"Certainly, do another culling. Do you have any plans for the dozen cowhands this winter?"

"Yes, one will repair harnesses, saddles and tack. One man will do maintenance on the agricultural implements. Four men will be hauling manure and fertilize our 400 acres reserved for crops. Two men will watch over the herd and ride the line for fence repairs. Four men will help Elliot build the new hay shed and your parent's home. And of course, the barn man has the entire remuda to care for and reshod every-one. The cook's work will stay the same."

"That settles it, the cowhands all stay on full payroll—no one gets furloughed. Now what are our plans for the spring."

"We're hoping for an easier calving season since crossbreed calves are usually smaller. That's ironic since they grow and profit much more than pure breeds. We are planning to castrate most of the bull calves since we want to harvest 2-year old steers for the market. Your purebred bulls will give service for another five years. We will select 20 more active crossbreed bull calves for breeding purposes two years from now. All pure-bred bull calves will also not be castrated, they will be kept for future sale. The one question is in regard to hot cauterizing calf's horn buds during the roundup."

"The practice is not clear to me, what's this about and what do you suggest."

"We are changing a herd of very long-horned animals to polled animals. The first-year crossbreeds will still produce horns, although not quite as long as the Texas Longhorns but still longer that the Durham Short Horns. If you want a polled herd, we'll need to hot cauterize the buds after branding the calves while we still have them secured."

"I see, how about if we don't cauterize the castrated bulls but cauterize the heifers and bulls grown for stock."

"Perfect."

"My last question relates to sequestering certain animals. What are you planning to do?"

"If we sequester the bulls from calving season to June, they become too aggressive. Left in the herd makes them more social and docile. Besides, a cow doesn't come in heat for almost two months after calving. What we really need to do is pull out one-year old heifers out of the herd and keep them in the separate paddocks till they are 18-24 months. Then introduce them to the herd in the June breeding season. This prevents premature breeding with its high calving mortality."

"Ok with me, my only concern with bulls left in the herd year-round is inbreeding. Can this become a genetic problem?"

"I realize that it's mathematically possible that a bull will end up breeding his mother, sister or daughter. The vet admits that this is theoretically a potential problem, but in reality, inbreeding occurs without bad offspring. This has been going on for hundreds of years because it's a logistical nightmare to try to separate cattle of the same lineage. I consider this a non-issue."

"The only other subject I have questions about is how we plan to supplement hay to 800 cattle this winter."

"Historically, we opened bales of hay in large piles and left the cattle to feed themselves willy-nilly. This led to much hay trampling and waste. Last year we built several bins with 30 degree slanted and slotted sides with a bottom tray 18 inches off the ground to catching droppings. That stopped trampling and the 8-month old calves had a much easier time to feed out of the bottom tray. So, for the next week, we'll build as many bins as possible. Our goal is to have 25—30 bins to handle 800 head of cattle."

"So, to summarize, the crossbreeding plan is in effect. Until the spring calving season arrives there is nothing else to plan, assuming the calving results are as expected, heh? Now do you have any questions?"

"One. You mentioned that you will continue participating in the US Marshal Service and that you will have periods you'll be away. Are you planning to commandeer some of the cowhands for deputy duty and or provide protection for Hannah during your absence?"

Hannah will be personally protected by my dad. As far as your cowhands, I'm not planning to turn them into lawmen. I will have three deputies assigned to me. I will take a seasoned Marshal from Colorado, a fresh greenhorn out of Lawman School and a local tracker— preferably an Indian."

"Oh shucks, there goes my barn man!"

"Your what?"

"You see, my barn man is an old Apache warrior by the name of Rocky. In reality, he and his squaw wife, Red Flower, take care of the barn and the horses. They live behind the barn in a tepee and are highly regarded by all the cowhands. Rocky was a well known tracker, by the name of Rock Wall, with his band of Apaches before the end of the Indian war in South Texas. He is also known as a speed shooter with the Winchester 73. Most important, you can trust him with your life. He would never abandon you."

"Thanks for the info, I'll speak to him. Were he to join me, could his wife take over while he's gone and how on earth did an Indian get such a name as Rocky?"

"No doubt, Red, as she is now known, would handle Rocky's duties. Now for Rocky's name. Remember how Indians were historically named—the chief would visit the newborn and upon stepping out of the teepee, the first thing he saw would be the baby's name. In the case of Rocky, the chief saw a rock wall and that became his name. After the Indian wars, he changed his name to a more American name and so he chose Rockwell. Working with cowhands who like nicknames, they started calling him Rocky and it stuck with him till today."

***

Over the next weeks, Jake and Hannah got into the swing of things. Hannah would take care of household duties, cook meals and care for the morning chicken coop duties. By 1PM, she started working on her studies and her typing. During the day, Jake would follow Clayton to learn the day by day activities of maintaining a ranch. By supper time the newlywed's lives rejoined. In the evening, they took care of gathering the chickens in the coop for nighttime security, gathering eggs and feeding the flock. Thereafter, they retired to their parlor for reading or talking.

It was that infamous evening when Jake said, "you realize Hannah that it's been a month since the trial, and we are now living in a rut of a pleasant and contented life. This will not continue at our age, and so I've come up with ten issues for us to discuss and come up to some agreement."

"Great, I'm all ears, please begin."

"The first is the 'crossbreeding program.' You're well aware of the short- and long-term plans. For now, everything depends on the calving season so let's table the subject for now."

"The second is the 'chicken enterprise.' For the short term, you've already stated you want to keep things the way they are. I agree, but in the long term several options will again come up. These are:"

- "We can increase egg production by only feeding layer pellets instead of 50/50 mash."

- "Egg production would also go up if we added 50 extra hens in each coop, especially if they are the new breed of layers called hybrids. One such hybrid is the Golden Comet which is known to produce 100 more eggs per year than a regular Rhode Island Red. Keep in mind that so much energy is needed to produce these extra eggs that their survival is half as long as any other layers."

- "A rotation schedule must be adhered to. My reading reveals that with 250 hens, a replacement of 50 birds per year is the absolute minimum since the 5-year old birds are now at 50% production when compared to one year old young hens."

- "At some point, we need to decide if we want to grow meat birds. These are hybrids with such names as Cornish Cross Hybrids, Brown Leghorn, Buckeye, and Chandelier. These are allowed to feed unrestricted and are kept in their coop. In 7 weeks, they are ready for market. With refrigeration coming onto the private sector, raising birds for meat has a profitable potential."

- "Eventually, we'll have to decide whether we wish to expand the private enterprise and go commercial. We are well situated to supply Austin and San Antonio by train freight. I hear thru the local cardboard company that disposable egg crates are about to come on the market. This would allow us to ship crates of individually packed dozens of eggs to outside markets. Of course, we would have to build extra coops or one mega coop. Something to consider, heh?" Hannah was thinking how this enterprise would interfere with her newfound hobby.

"The third issue is 'the Marshal Service.'" Hannah took over and said, "take the district leadership position. Get yourself three deputies, set up an office in the New Braunfels courthouse. Let the deputies handle federal processes, serve Judge Hobart, and only get involved in manhunts, transferring dangerous prisoners, and protecting the judge from death threats. It's no longer an issue of contention. I love you too much to try to control your life, I won't be a shrew or a dominatrix. Moving on!"

"The fourth issue is 'construction.' Cass will start building my parents' house, barn and windmill well this week. I think we should extend the cabin. The Newmanns need more room and luxury. I propose we extend the kitchen and add a scullery. With running water, we'll purchase them a manually operated washing machine." Hannah added, "and of course, let's buy one washing machine for my scullery, heh?"

"The fifth issue is the 'crop farm.' You already know about expanding 100 acres, hiring homesteader young men, and adding a hay shed, baler, and oat's thresher. What you don't know about is the fact I'm planning to go commercial and sell hay in San Antonio and Austin. To do this, we're going to need a train siderail going to the baler platform." Hannah added, "how are you going to make that happen?" "I have a secret weapon, a high-up railroad executive who owes me a favor! Just go with it for now."

"The sixth issue is 'oil.' I plan to dig a test well which would cost me approximately $10,000. Or, I could let an oil giant like Standard Oil dig a well, and if it comes in, I would take a royalty per barrel of crude. If it doesn't come in, I lose nothing. What do you think we should do?" Hannah thought about it and said, "let's wait and see how much of your time is spent as a US Marshal before deciding."

"The seventh one is the 'Klaus ranch.' The adopted son, Dieter, has taken over. He's selling all the cattle, firing the cowhands and moving his oil drilling rigs to the ranch. He's going to go into the oil business big time. He'll need more cash than the value of the cattle sale, so the word is that he'll lease the homesteader farms for an extended period, but he's reserving all mineral and oil rights. What do you know of this man?" Hannah answered, "he's a real popinjay!"

"Whoa, what is a popinjay?" "It's a person who is arrogant, extravagant, conceited and a real snob. He'll talk down to you, so if you have any dealings with him, make sure that the conditions are in your favor. He has been a master of one-ups-Manship."

"Well, in this regard, we come to item eight, 'more real-estate.' Our immediate neighbor to the east is a homestead with a half section of 320 acres. Clayton has checked it out, and the acreage borders the main road and appears very fertile. I think we should try to lease it for 20 years or longer and plant more hay crops. Plus, Willie could live in the house and use the barn. Were he to marry, we would give him enough land to have a garden and a small pasture for his horses." "Yes, we can have our lawyer write up a lease that protects us. Besides, I like the idea of Willie living nearby."

"Item nine is 'Clayton.' I've always believed that a crucial employee must be well compensated to keep him around. Just to let you know, he's getting married soon and I can't afford to lose him if I'm going to be gone doing Marshal duties. So, I've doubled his salary and we're going to build him a small house next to our barn. Plus, his wife wants to work the crop farming business." "Wow, good for you. That's one hell of an incentive to stick around."

"The tenth item is a hot one—you need a 'chicken farm' worker. We've talked about you spending the afternoon studying, typing and writing. To do this, you need help. There is too much to do in the coop and garden. We need to hire a retired homesteader couple who lives in town and is willing to work 1-5PM daily six days a week. During their time here, they would take care of the garden, grind up vegetables to feed, pick up eggs, change the wood shavings and bring in the brood before leaving. That way, the brood will have two hours to lay eggs. We'll feed them at 7PM before it gets dark. What do you think?" "I've been to four classes so far, and my instructor acknowledges that my progress is ahead of the class because I spend four hours a day at it. Yes, I want some help, and we'll increase both coops with 50 Hybrid Golden Comet to help pay for the employees."

"Well, those are my ten issues. Do you have anything to bring up?"

"Yes, every time I go outside to get some kindling or cook-stove wood, it's wet and hard to fire up. Could we build a woodshed attached to the back-kitchen door. I'm sure the Newmanns have the same problem." "Of course, we'll have Cass build two woodsheds that can hold three cords of wood—one cord of cookstove wood, one pallet of kindling wood, and the balance in heating firewood. We'll have the firewood company deliver and stack the wood with a walkway between the two types of wood. Is that it?"

"Well, according to Helga Wolfgang, did you know that Willie has a lady friend who works as a chambermaid at the Zimmerman Hotel?"

"No, I didn't know. Now I know how he spent his time, when we told him to entertain himself till we met at the sheriff's office at 3PM. Good for him, I hope it works out."

"Anything else?"

"Yes, what happens with all these plans if I get pregnant?"

"Whoa, that changes everything, since having a child trumps all these plans. What happened when you saw Doc Craven? All you said was that you were normal. Heck, I could have told you that. So, is there any more to share?"

"Yes, it appears that my monthlies are irregular because I don't regularly ovulate. Which makes it difficult to get pregnant."

"Is there a treatment for this problem?"

"Yes, it's called getting pregnant. After the full pregnancy and birth, the ovaries will tend to be more regular.

"Wow, now that's a real dilemma. Can't get

pregnant but need to get pregnant to solve the problem."

"Yes, Doc Craven admitted it was a catch 22 situation."

"Well, one day you can explain that phrase. For now, all we can do is to continue our love making and hope for the best. Either way, with our love, WE'LL MANAGE, heh!"

**

The End

AUTHOR'S NOTE

The end of Chapter 12 provides ten short- and long-term plans that can flow into another story. The lead events include the life and times of a US Marshal team in South Texas, the crossbreeding experiment, oil drilling, commercial egg production and a burgeoning writer.

The difference between these two books is the time frame. One is in the 19th century and the second starts creeping in the early industrial 20th century. Yet the hero and heroine interactions continue with a romantic and comedic twist.

If you enjoyed this current publication, leave comments on Amazon. These comments not only help sales, but they reassure new readers of the class of western fiction. For your enjoyment, look for a sequel to follow.

Printed in the United States
By Bookmasters